Moreno Valley
Public Library
25480 Alessandro Blvd
Moreno Valley, CA
92553

D0486265

NO. AR.

DEXTER'S
FOOTBALL
JOURNAL

BY

E. J. MANN

1

Dexter's Football Journal copyright 2014 belongs to Emma Wood.

Cover copyright 2014 belongs to Emma Wood.

All rights reserved.

This book is a work of fiction and any resemblance of characters or plot to actual persons or actual events is purely coincidental.

The moral right of the author has been asserted.

This book is sold subject to the condition that it shall not be reproduced or copied without the author's consent.

This book is for my children,

Matthew and Rachel.

May you achieve all your life goals.

Moreno Valley Public Library

Mirano Valley Public Library

August 2011

Kick Off

The Super League's new season has kicked off at last!

I don't know why Mum and my little sister Melissa groaned when I mentioned that *Super League Scorers* would be returning to our screens tonight. Mum records it for me, much to Melissa's dismay. Since it starts at ten o'clock, which is past my bedtime.

It's the best start to the day EVER, when I catch it at 6.30 am.

Six thirty is my standard waking up time.

I have been known to get up even earlier when I'm excited about something. That morning, I was so delighted by the prospect of a whole new footie season that I woke at 5.23 am.

No way was I returning to sleep when Fabio was waiting for me on my television screen.

I sneaked downstairs. And watched him smash the Super Kickers out of the match with a 6–4 win.

Start as you mean to go on, Fabio!

I was so relieved when Fabio was selected as captain of the Super Strikers for yet another season.

So was Mum, since it meant we didn't have to change my bedroom decor.

Fabio's been on blazing form over the past year. He was top scorer in the Scottish Premier League last season.

Achieving no less than 38 goals.

A slight calf injury set him back for a few weeks in March this year. But he soon bounced back. Perhaps due to his healthy Mediterranean diet. I am researching footballer's diets at the end of this month as part of my overall football training.

Active mind, active body. Or that's the plan.

Fabio's parents are Spanish but have lived in Edinburgh since the 1980's, when his Dad came to work for a Scottish oil company. Fabio was born in this bonnie land.

I am so grateful that Fabio was lured to my stunning homeland, Scotland. Now he just needs to be lured to the equally stunning ME!

Melissa was still in bed when I watched my favourite football programme. So she missed the torture - *as she puts it* - of watching a bunch of burly blokes kicking a ball around.

Mel and I take turns to watch our TV choices in the mornings. When Mum and Dad have a long-lie (say to seven o'clock) or are in their morning showers.

It's not my fault that Melissa's children's programmes last twenty minutes. While *Super League Scorers* lasts for an hour and a half.

One choice each is still fair.

Melissa is my annoying little sister.

The most annoying thing about Melissa is that she is **NOT** a boy. And she does **NOT** like football.

She is 6 years old and detests most sports that I love to watch. Football, rugby, snooker, alpine skiing, diving... anything with a winner at the end basically.

Melissa has long, straight brown hair that she doesn't like being brushed. So it is mostly pushed back from her face by a headband. I wish Melissa had been born a boy. Then I would have a cool brother to practise football with in the garden. I would place him in goals and take penalties for hours on end. Until he was trained as an expert goalie.

Unlike my rubbish sister who lets everything in.

The neighbour's cat wandering past the goal stands a better chance than Melissa of preventing me scoring.

It was brilliant to see the best football league in the world get off to such a cracking start.

Fabio scored a hat trick!

In his debut match of the season, Fabio performed a fabulous header.

The Super Kicker's goalie was practically on his nose in a vain attempt to save it.

Fabio then scored a wonderful bullet-shot penalty goal. Awarded as a result of a disgraceful foul by one of the Super Kicker's best defenders.

Who was promptly sent off.

Thus the barrage of goals from the Strikers.

Super League matches are usually far more evenly balanced. Since both teams are of an equally high standard.

Finally, Fabio scooped the ball into the left-hand corner of the net. Thanks to a sweeping corner pass from his team-mate Wilson.

This completed his trio of blazing-hot goals.

What a thrilling opening match.

**Final score of August Match:
Super Strikers v Super Kickers 6-4**

All About Me

I train faithfully every day to ensure that *I* become a Super League player as soon as I am old enough to qualify, which is at sixteen.

August got off to a cracking start for me too.

I managed an impressive tally of four goals throughout August whilst playing for my school team, Eastwood Rovers. Unfortunately my arch rival, Taylor Bradley scored five goals. Placing him ahead of me in the title race to become top scorer in the Edinburgh Schools' Football League.

Rumour is rife that TB is not a real-life boy. But a goal–scoring robot. Created to test fellow teammate's drive and determination.

I have vowed to increase my training regime next month in a bid to knock TB off the top spot.

(Which I wouldn't mind doing literally as well as metaphorically.)

Here's a little information about my footballing life: -

Name: Dexter Hunter

Age: 10 years old.

Follow: Scottish Super League. It's made up of the elite Scottish football players. Matches are played once a month throughout the season. Players are split into two teams: the Super Strikers and Super Kickers. At the end of the season, the *Super League Star Player* is selected by public vote - winning a medal and £100,000 prize money. The winning team is presented with the famous Super League trophy. All games sell out within two hours of ticket release.

Favourite Footballer: Fabio Galianto. Captain of the Super Strikers. Top scorer in the Super League for the last 3 years.

My Football Team: Eastwood Rovers. Play in the Edinburgh School Football League.

Goals Scored: 42 goals last season. Joint top scorer (*with Taylor Bradley*). Must score at least 50 this year to win title outright.

Season's Goal: Persuade Fabio Galianto to become my coach, companion and father-figure by the end of the season.

Life Goal: Become a professional footballer and be selected to play in the Super League, like Fabio.

In order to achieve my **Season's Goal** and **Life Goal**, I follow Fabio's words of wisdom. Fabio said in a recent interview that to become a member of the Super League you need:-

1. **Natural talent** (GOT)
2. **Expert coaching (NEED)**
3. **Ambition and dreams** (GOT)
4. **Follow all matches avidly** (YES)
5. **Practise, Practise, Practise** (YES, YES, YES)

I am naturally blessed with **1 and 3**.

I thoroughly enjoy **4 and 5** - on a regular basis.

However, I would like **FABIO** to help me out with **Requirement Number 2**... I need Fabio to become my super-star coach and all round father-figure. To guide me to footballing stardom as soon as possible.

That is my current season's goal and I plan to complete it by the end of the season.

Top Fan

I believe that Fabio and I are so alike that we must come from the same gene-pool.

All I have to do is orchestrate a meeting with Fabio. So that *he* gets a chance to realise we are cut from the same cloth.

Of course, I already have a dad, who does play football with me whenever cajoled into it. But I don't think even *he* would class himself as a top coach. Plus Dad works away from home in Manchester (but is not a Man United or Man City fan thankfully).

This means that Dad is only available at weekends. So he misses my all important football training on a Monday night and can NEVER play footie in the garden with me after work like a lot of my friends' dads do.

Dad has short, black hair which he chooses not to spike up for some reason. He enjoys wearing thick woollen jumpers a great deal of the time.

Well, it is a bit chilly up here in Scotland.

And they are very comfy to cuddle against.

Dad sports thin, circular silver-rimmed glasses. Not unlike Harry Potter's round shaped ones. Except his were black, of course.

Dad seems to nod off on the couch a lot whilst reading his newspaper.

It's all that travelling to and from Manchester, he says.

Not that I let him get much rest.

If I see him dozing off and doing anything as boring as sleep during the day (it's bad enough going to sleep at bedtime) I save him by dragging him into the garden to play sport with me.

I am very thoughtful like that.

Ever since Fabio Galianto first qualified to play in the Super League in 2009, I have loved him as much as any boy could love a parent.

Obviously he's not had the chance to love me back yet, as he has never met me.

Or indeed heard of me.

My best mate Mikey has decided that the best strategy to get Fabio to notice me is to score an extraordinary amount of goals for my school team, Eastwood Rovers.

Then, I will get my name in all of the local newspapers.

Then, Fabio can find out about me and claim me as his very own protégée to love, nourish and train.

Mikey reckons football scouts are everywhere. Reporting back to all the top teams about young talent. My aim is to get picked up by the Scottish Football Development Agency.

They receive 20% of the Super League seats. So that alone would improve my chances of seeing Fabio in the flesh.

Needless to say I was at my computer the minute match tickets were released at 9 am on Friday 1st August.

Frustratingly, I had no luck achieving any precious seats for this year's matches.

Apparently tickets sold out in a record 9.1 seconds this year.

<u>Reasons I Love Fabio</u>

The Top Ten reasons I love Fabio and want him to become my coach/companion/father-figure are:-

1. Fabio is the Super League's all time highest scorer. Fabio scored a total of 27 goals last season for his Super League team. There are only 10 games per season (one a month between August and May) so that's nearly a hat trick a match. What a legend!

2. His hair looks mega-cool and is black and spiky just like mine. Only my hair is more of a mousy brown colour.

3. He is Spanish and I love going to Spain on holidays. Since I get to eat ice lollies every day and play football beside the pool, trying not to hit any sunbathers in the face with my ball. *Not always successfully.*

4. Fabio is a bona fide legend. It would be nice to have a footie legend, instead of an accountant, for a dad.

5. I am able to speak excellent Spanish, just like Fabio. My excellent Spanish word is hola which means hello. And so is very useful. I'm sure Fabio would be able to teach me lots of other useful Spanish words. Such as goal, off-side, penalty and captain. And most usefully, Dexter Hunter is top scorer of the Edinburgh Schools' Football League. Although Dexter Hunter would still be Dexter Hunter in Spanish, of course.

6. Fabio would be able to take me to my football training sessions every Monday AND play football with me in the garden every day after work. Since professional footballers finish training at midday – result!

7. With Fabio training me on a **daily** basis I would easily manage to beat the football machine, Taylor Bradley and become Eastwood Rover's top scorer. (I would happily give up school and dedicate my entire life to football but I doubt Mum and Dad would allow it.)

8. Fabio, as a father-figure, could live with us if he wanted to and guide me in the world of football.

9. Once Fabio knew how excellent my football skills were, from all our family time together, he would be sure to put my name forward for a coaching programme for talented youngsters. Then I wouldn't have to worry about talent scouts failing to spot my top skills.

10. Fabio could help me with my research projects examining aspects of the beautiful game. My walking, talking encyclopaedia of footballing information would be with me at all times. Perfect.

I could go on with the reasons I love Fabio but I'll stop at ten.

<u>Rivals</u>

Unfortunately my plan to become top scorer for Eastwood Rovers is not quite going to plan.

Taylor Bradley is already two clear goals ahead of me.

Drat!

At school Taylor Bradley is known by his initials –
TB.

TB is the name of an infectious, disgusting, deadly disease. So is very fitting.

TB is the tallest boy in our class, P6c at Eastwood Primary School in South Edinburgh.

He boasts chunky calves and muscular arms from all the swimming that he does.

He insists on bringing into school all the medals that he wins for his swimming.

None of us are remotely interested in a sport that does not even involve a ball.

TB has black flat, floppy hair that always looks like it needs a good cut.

His mouth seems to smirk rather than smile when speaking to people. He's not at all popular in the classroom or in the playground. But he's always the first to be selected for gym games.

Cue yet more smirks from his mealy mouth.

I've decided to increase my daily training regime until Fabio arrives on the scene as my coach and knight in shining armour.

(Or latest Super League footie kit, more likely.)

Hopefully this will be enough to pip TB to the top spot next month.

<u>Golden Opportunity</u>

My best friend, Mikey McMillan, came round to my house to practise football on Monday before training, as usual. He arrived once he had eaten all of his dinner and completed his homework - his mum's rules - at 5.33 pm. It was our first day back at football training in the new school year.

Spiky Mikey is the best mate any boy could hope for. He has blonde, cool, spiky hair, blue eyes and lots of freckles. Mikey adores football almost as much as me.

We always ask for the same football strips for our birthdays. So that we will be matching at training sessions, playing football in the park, our gardens, going to football birthday parties - at all times possible, basically.

Mikey reckons matching outfits improves our alliance. Leading to better passes. And hopefully more goals.

He's very switched on is Mikey!

We usually head straight to my back garden to get a few practise kicks in before training kicks off at 6 o'clock. This time Mikey whispered to me to go upstairs to my room to talk tactics. He'd a top move up his sleeve, regarding my mission to make Fabio my coach.

I think Mikey's worked out that since he's my best mate and plays football at my house practically every day after school. He's in for a lot of extra coaching by Fabio too!

"You'll never believe what's in the latest issue of *GOAL Magazine.*" Mikey pulled the comic out of his football kit bag and handed it to me. "Check out page twenty-seven."

"Cheers, Mikey. I love this magazine," I said as I thumbed through the pages to the one Mikey suggested.

I tried not to get distracted en route by the amazing headlines and cool pictures of all the top players.

I wondered what poster Mikey had spotted – must be one of Fabio.

I couldn't believe my sight when I saw the headline on page twenty-seven.

Bold as anything, the words jumped off the page-

"WIN VIP TICKETS TO SEE THE SUPER LEAGUE'S 100ᵗʰ MATCH LIVE AT HAMPDEN STADIUM."

The lucky winner will receive TWO VIP tickets to visit Hampden Stadium. To witness the Super League's 100th match on 31st January 2012.

The exciting match will be followed by a commemorative performance by top Scottish band, *Cool Dudes.*

All to mark the Super League reaching its centenary match.

"What a spot, Mikey! We can finally get our mucky hands on some sell-out tickets. Be yards from Fabio. VIP seats to boot!"

I was so excited.

Mikey and I began jumping up and down on my Super League-covered bedspread, shrieking with delirium. Until we were gasping for breath.

Must improve fitness levels.

Mum hollered up the stairs to stop bouncing about on the bed. We were making the ceiling on the room below shake apparently.

"I couldn't believe it when I spotted it," Mikey agreed.

Once we'd recovered our composure, Mikey pointed out the front cover to me.

It had a glorious picture of none other than my beloved Fabio with the words:-

"TWO TICKETS TO SEE LEGEND FABIO GALIANTO ON HIS HOME TURF."

"This magazine usually has hardly any Scottish football in it," said Mikey.

"I know," I agreed.

I liked the cover picture of Fabio so much that Mikey kindly let me tear it out and stick it on my wall.
I positioned it in the middle of my four Man of the Match cards. That I was awarded last season from Eastwood Rovers.

So I was completely surrounded Fabio. We were like one happy - not to mention successful - team.

Later that night I ran off five copies of the picture to cover all my school jotters with. When Mum went to use the printer at the weekend, I heard her complaining that someone had used up all the red ink.

Oops!

I gazed at my new poster and kept imagining myself cheering on Fabio. With all the other Super Strikers fans live at Hampden stadium.
From my starry VIP front row seat.
I pictured Fabio waving at me from the pitch and shouting, *"Dexter, great to finally meet you!"*
It was only as I saw myself excitedly shouting back to Fabio, that he should become my star coach as soon as possible, that I realised I didn't know what was required to actually win this prize.

"What've we got to do to secure these precious babies?" I enquired.

My mind flipped back to reality and my fingers to page twenty-seven to find out.

"That's the tough bit. You've got to *draw* a picture of your favourite footballer on his summer holidays," Mikey groaned.

I physically winced at the word **draw**.

*I'm known for my **football** not **artistic** skills!*

I quickly scanned page twenty-seven until I found an explanation of the competition at the very bottom of the page.
I read it out to Mikey. Even though I knew he'd already looked at it and knew what was involved.

The article said-

"Draw a picture of your favourite Super League player as you imagine him having fun on his holidays.
The picture must be A4 size.
You may use any art materials that you wish.
Good luck to all you creative Super League fans out there!

This is your chance to win sell out tickets to the centenary match of a lifetime"

<u>Competition Entry</u>

Mikey gave me a knowing look.

He knew how bad I was at art.

After a few concerned glances between me and Mikey, I decided it was not sportsman like to be defeatist.

"How hard can this be? We'll draw a picture of Fabio on holiday right here in *Scotland.* One of the most beautiful places on earth after all. Where else would he want to go? Especially when his son-in-waiting lives here! Everyone else will choose to draw a sunny place so our entry will stand out," I suggested.

"That's a good idea, Dex. The Super League powers-that-be will like it. They're always complaining that the Scottish matches don't get the same coverage as the English ones."

In the end we both agreed that this was too good an opportunity to pass up.

I should at least have a go. Mikey kindly agreed to help me. Well, it was TWO tickets on offer after all.

I didn't like to point out that he was almost as bad at drawing as me.

We decided to make a 3D image.
This was very on-trend at the cinema and would hopefully make our entry leap of the page. Literally as well as in the minds of the judges. The rules stated that you could use any form of art materials that you wished.
The 3D picture took us *AGES* to complete.
We had no time to practise football before training that night.

Or play football on Tuesday after school.

Or play footie on Wednesday after school.

Or even have a kick around on Thursday after school.

Mikey and I finally finished our masterpiece late on Friday afternoon.

By this time Mum was considering taking me to see the doctor, concerned that I was seriously ill.

I had not been out in my own back garden once all week which was most unlike me.
Mum thought that I must be coming down with something serious.
Thankfully I persuaded her to leave it until Monday to see how I was. I calmly reassured her that I had simply been busy in my room, with Mikey, researching Fabio's recent form.

She didn't realise I meant literally, of course.

Mikey and I glued some white A4 computer paper onto the back of an empty cereal box. (Well, it was empty one I had stuffed the remaining wheat flakes into Melissa's chocolate pops box. Much to her surprise when she went to get her usual sugary start to the day the next morning and found a healthier alternative poured out.) This made a solid, impressive canvas, we thought.

We then cut out pieces of string and glued them onto our blank canvas to comprise the goal's net.

Mikey had the bright idea of sticking on one of my ping pong balls as the football.

I then painstakingly copied the cover picture of Fabio from Mikey's *GOAL Magazine*.

I drew him wear a kilt, holding a plate of haggis in one hand and a can of Irn Bru, Scotland's favourite fizzy drink, in the other. I drew tartan football boots on his feet, which were expertly kicking the ping pong ball in the direction of the string goal.

The backdrop of our masterpiece was all coloured a dark grey-blue colour for the sky.

We then carefully stuck on lots of blobs of blue play dough, from Melissa's play dough set, to signify rain.

Scotland is not known for its good weather.

Even as harsh critics of our own artistic talents, both Mikey and I thought the end result was extremely original and a good likeness of Fabio.

I gave Mikey my best football trading card as a thank you for letting me enter the competition in *my* name. It was *his* magazine after all. So he could have entered in *his* name if he wanted to.

He's such a top mate.

I gave him, as a freebie, my Wayne Rooney Hundred Club Shiny Limited Edition card (which had 114 Attack and 102 Defence scores).

It was a worthy swap for the chance to see Fabio play live with my best pal in the whole world.

I gently placed the competition entry into a large brown padded envelope, from the packet of padded envelopes kept in the spare room.

Mum uses them for sending birthday gifts to our cousins in England. I then wrote the address on the front of the envelope in neat capital letters.

It was 5.52 pm on Friday evening by the time we were finished.

Phew.

Mum hollered up the stairs that it was time for Mikey to go home. Dad would be arriving from Manchester soon.

We always order a take-out pizza for dinner on a Friday to celebrate Dad coming home and prevent Mum having to cook.

I have pepperoni pizza and share a large size with Dad. Melissa chooses ham topping and shares a medium size with Mum. Mikey knows all about our Friday Pizza Dinner Ritual so gets ready to head off.

He often stays for tea on other nights, so doesn't mind at all.

Mikey and I were both chuffed with ourselves for finishing the entry. And making such a brilliant job of it. Considering we were both hopeless at art.

Hidden talents lurked beneath our Super Striker strips obviously.

<u>Payback Time</u>

Once Mikey had his shoes and coat on, we showed Mum the competition envelope.

We asked if we could post it in the post-box while walking Mikey home.

Mum said our envelope was too chunky to fit in the post-box.

She would need to walk to the Post Office tomorrow to post it she said.

She did not look too thrilled at this prospect.

So we, finally, confessed to Mum all about *GOAL Magazine's* thrilling competition. We told her how hard we had worked on the 3D drawing. We explained how magnificent the prize was.

Then, Mum softened.

She was impressed that we had been working so hard on an arts and crafts project. We must have been super keen on the prize, Mum observed, to spend every day after school on it. Not much holds us back from playing football in the garden each night.

She also muttered something about her precious plants having had a welcome chance to recover from all our stray balls.

Mum dutifully posted our entry at the Post Office while Melissa was at her Saturday morning ballet class the next day, as agreed. Later on she told me that the padded envelope counted as a Large Parcel and had cost £4.75 to send.

That was more than my weekly pocket money allowance of £3 per week. Even though I argued that my pocket money should be raised to £5 a week, the same as Mikey got. Mum refused such an increase. She insisted most people she knew still only gave their kids one pound a week in pocket money.

Mum obviously has some very stingy friends.

To keep the peace. And ensure Mum didn't take the £1.75 out of next week's pocket money. Leaving me without enough money to buy *my* favourite magazine – *Scottish League Success Stories* - I agreed to water all her plants. Front and back garden. For a week. As payment for the surplus.

Mum seemed quite pleased with this deal.

She loves to keep her garden looking immaculate.

Especially the front garden which all the neighbours can see. Personally, I can't understand why anyone would choose to spend time in the garden watering boring plants, pulling up slimy weeds and spraying a dirty path clear of moss. When they could be having fun practising penalties or improving their ball control skills.

But each to their own.

I didn't mind watering Mum's plants for the week.

We have quite a big back garden and a long rectangular front garden so it counts as good exercise.

Great training for my future life as a fit, famous, footballer's son!

That's if I can ever get Fabio to know I exist...

August Research Topic

Top Footballers' Diet Facts

1. When Arsene Wenger became manager of Arsenal Football club in 1996 he changed the diet of his team. They had been eating a lot of fried and sugary foods **(not unlike me)**. Wenger believed the team's poor diet was affecting their performance on the pitch. He introduced a low fat, high fibre diet, with lots of fish, chicken and vegetables **(Mum would approve of his views!)**. Arsenal has been on top form recently. So I think Arsene Wenger may be onto something...

2. Professional footballers' diets should include high quantities of quality carbohydrates (wholegrain bread, cereal, fruit and vegetables). This provides their body with enough energy to run, dodge and tackle on the field for 90 minutes. In addition they require protein (from eggs, nuts, chicken and fish) to assist the body's recovery from all the rigours of exercise.

Out with my post-match unhealthy bag of crisps then!

3. The Mediterranean diet has been shown to have numerous health benefits. Including reducing heart disease and cancer. (Spain is in the Mediterranean so I think Fabio may follow this diet.) It involves eating only a little red meat, lots of fruit and vegetables, quality proteins, whole grains and using oil rather than butter.

I shall ask Mum to commence following this diet immediately for me.

4. Footballers burn a nigh number of calories per game. You would think that would leave loads of room for treats. *Unfortunately treats are out, I'm afraid!* Professional footballers, to remain in peak fitness and health, should avoid processed food and foods high in sugar or fat, as these will sap the body's energy. *Shame.*

5. **Water**. Players need plenty of hydration before, during and after training sessions and matches. Young players, such as me, require even more drinks as they do not sweat as much as adults.

<u>Action plan –</u>

1. Drop the bag of crisps that I eat in the car on the way home from training.
2. Have two bowls of cereal instead of one for breakfast.
3. Fill my water bottle to the very top before training and make sure that I finish it all.
4. Ask Mum to use olive oil instead of butter on my sandwiches in my lunch box.
5. Only have one unhealthy snack a week. (This will not be easy with temptation all around me. Especially at the school's tuck shop which has lovely homemade cookies!)

<u>September 2011</u>

"A succession of stunning saves by the Striker's goalie, plus a late goal from Fabio, meant the Strikers scraped their second win of the season."

September Super League Result:
Super Strikers v Super Kickers 1 – 0

Overall Result: 2 - 0 to the Strikers

<u>My Results</u>

Replies to Competition: 0

Goals Scored:
8 this month. Bringing my total to 14. TB's current tally is 13.

Personal training:
10 penalty shoot outs
15 keepy-uppies
30 push ups, and
10 laps of back garden per day.

September Research Topic:
Football Training Drills

Commentary

The Super League match was disappointing this month.

It remained goalless until 89 minutes.

Thankfully, at this nail bitingly late stage, Fabio managed to find the back of the net.

The Super Kickers came out fighting with a succession of near misses. One of which clipped the right-hand post – very worrying.

My stomach lurched to my throat when I thought the Kickers were about to take the lead from Fabio - for the first time this season...

It was only thanks to three fabulous saves by the wonderful Super Striker goalkeeper that the Super Kickers failed to notch up their first victory.

Fabio's late goal secured a second win for his team who at least can say they remain undefeated.

Thus far...

A close one.

Family Support

I had a rather uncomfortable conversation with Dad on the way home from my first Eastwood Rovers football match of the month.

A super - embarrassing experience with Dad at a football match followed later that week.

I will explain all.

Dad always drives me to and from football, on a Saturday morning, in our silver Volkswagen people carrier. Most of the seven available seats are never used, in our minibus-style car, since Melissa and I only require two back seats. But Mum and Dad like the tranquillity the extra space provides.

Dad likes to use this travel time for *our special little chats*. On this particular Saturday (3rd September) our discussion did not commence well.

Eastwood Rover's football match was over and we had won 8-5.

I had been on top form. I'd managed to score two stunning goals as well as setting up a beauty for Mikey.

Despite all this, Dad's face was glum.

He spoke to me in that flat-toned voice parents use when they are angry.

But are trying not to give the game away and actually sound angry.

"Dex, Mum told me about the letter you'd written to Fabio," Dad finally offloaded as he drove out the training ground. Still trying to act casual, he added, "I can see why you'd want Fabio to be your coach. But in your letter you said you wanted him to be your *DAD* as well. What's that all about son?"

Dad looked very hurt indeed.

I'd already been through all this with Mum when she found the letter. I couldn't believe she'd shopped me to Dad.

Especially in view of what I had written.

I explained to Dad, "I've already told Mum. It's not that you're not a great dad. It's just that you're always away at work. You miss my Monday training sessions *every* week. I just want a dad that's around all the time. Like normal dads are."

I knew I sounded sulky.

"I know it's not ideal me working away, Dexy. But someone's got to pay for all your football gear. Lessons, kit, boots, comics... Not to mention the countless balls lost over the fence needing replaced. It all costs money!"
"I know Dad and I appreciate it. Honest I do. It's just that Fabio is so cool. And has such brilliant, spiky hair. I just want *him* to coach me. So I can become a

super star like him! I only meant father *figure*. In a *watching-over-my-football-skills* kind of a way." I faltered, trying to gain some ground.

For some reason Dad found this funny.

I knew he could not query the issue of Fabio's hair being super-cool.

Dad was NOT lucky in the hair department.
He was not *so* unlucky that he was bald or anything... But Dad's hair just flops down against his head. Even when it's just been cut and should look smart.

As I thought, the hair card worked.

Dad said, "Let's just forget about it then. But remember, Dex. I'm only working away because I lost my job in Edinburgh. When there were lots of redundancies at my office. I'm keeping my eye out for jobs closer to home. There's nothing I'd like more than to take you to Monday football training every week."
"It would be so cool if you were home every night to save me from living in an all girls' house!"
Dad laughed as he pulled up at the local Burger Bar for our traditional Saturday post-match lunch together.

(The healthy eating plan detailed in August will not apply to Saturdays. Everything in moderation.)

"There's nothing wrong with Mum and Melissa."
Dad gave me a sly wink.

I decided not to disagree since I was on a yellow card. The last thing I wanted was a red card and to be sent home without my scrummy cheeseburger and chips for lunch.

I was annoyed that Mum had told Dad about the letter. I'd given it to her to post on Thursday night. I must have left the envelope unsealed.

Mum read my PRIVATE letter WITHOUT my permission.

She then had the cheek to blast *me* for not being grateful for my wonderful, caring, supportive, hard-working dad.

It was only when I explained to Mum about Fabio's many sporting and hair-related attributes that she seemed to calm down.

I think deep down Mum knew Dad could not compete with a Premier League footballing legend.

Mum joked that she wouldn't mind trying life as a WAG (**W**ife **and G**irlfriend of a footballer) for a bit! She could get used to all the designer handbags, beauty treatments and five-star holidays apparently.

I had specifically asked Mum **NOT** to tell Dad.

Despite Mum insisting that I always do as I am told. She did NOT do as she was told. And blabbed to Dad immediately!

Parents – who'd have them?

The letter took a lot of time and effort to compose. Luckily Mikey was there to help me. We were meant to be researching Vikings for our school project. But it wasn't due until next Friday. So we decided to put our time to better use.

The letter read –

Dear Fabio,

I think you are fab, just like your name!

I am 10 years old and am your biggest fan in the whole world, certainly the whole of Edinburgh.

I am currently top scorer for my school football team, Eastwood Rovers. Just like you were the Super League's top scorer last season. I have applied to a competition to try and win tickets to see you play

January's Super League match so maybe I'll get to meet you soon!

I'm writing to ask you if you would be interested in becoming my coach and even my dad if you want to be. The main reasons that I think you should become my coach/father figure are that we both love football, both have spiky hair, both train every day, both score lots of goals, both do clean passes and both live in Edinburgh.

Imagine the fun we would have and what a lot we already have in common - we'd be like an instant family to each other.

Please contact me right away. Please send me a signed photograph. If you want to include a signed football strip or football as a treat for me, that would lovely.

In fact, you can send anything you like, as long as you reply.

Love, Dexter xxx

P.S. If you wish to mention me being the top scorer at Eastwood Rovers to the Scottish Football Development Agency that would be fine.

As Dad and I munched on our 100%-beef burgers with cheese and barbeque sauce, Dad remarked that not many Spaniards like Fabio had sons with pale skin with freckles and that spoke with a Scottish accent.

I knew he was just jealous.

Dad's Star Move

I've been checking the post every day for a reply to my competition entry.

Still nothing.

The entries had to be in by 31st August so admittedly I've not given the magazine long to consider all the drawings. But I'm hoping mine will stand out so much (hopefully for the right reasons) that their decision will be quick and easy. Just like scoring against Melissa at football.

On Saturday afternoon, after lunch, Dad spent the entire time hogging the computer.

Presumably researching Fabio's cool hairstyle to see if there is any way he could copy it and impress his son.

That evening however it turned out Dad had thought of an even better way to impress me.

At ten past eight when Melissa was safely tucked up in bed - her bedtime is seven o'clock and mine is nine o'clock since I'm older than her - Dad announced that he had an exciting surprise for me. He looked a tad excited himself.

I was relieved that he'd lost his gloomy look from earlier.

"I think you're right, Dexy. We do need to spend more time together. Life's been all about *work, work, work* lately. Travelling to *work* and from *work*..."

I got bored at the mention of Dad's *work* and started to switch off. Then Dad shocked me with a surprise side-tackle move.

"After hours of trawling the internet, I've found out about a father and son football tournament. It's on at our local sports centre tomorrow. I've put our names down, Dex!"

I tried to move my mouth into an upward position resembling smile whilst internally screaming,

"Nooooooooooooooooooooooooooooooo!"

Dad's terrible at football and is so un-cool.

He will totally embarrass me.

"Dad, that's so sweet of you to think of something we can do together. But I've swimming lessons on a Sunday. Remember?"

Thank goodness for swimming being an essential activity for my own safety. As Mum and Dad are always telling me!

"It's okay just his once, Dex. Nothing is as important as US!"

Dad gave me a sincere smile and ruffled my hair (destroying my cool spikes).

I was cornered.

"Super." I managed, weakly.

This is going to be so humiliating.

Football Tournament

Sunday afternoon came about all too quickly.

I've never been as slow to get my football kit on for a match in all my life, Mum remarked. As Dad hollered up the stairs that it was time to go.

The match started in half an hour.

I made my way down the stairs with a sinking feeling which only worsened at the sight of Dad.

He was wearing his one and only football strip - a ten years out of date Spanish strip.

The shirt looked at least two sizes too small for him and accentuated a circular belly shape around Dad's middle. The shorts looked perhaps three sizes too small and clung to his thighs like cycling shorts. Dad obviously lost or never owned the matching socks. So he had put on his work grey socks.

Dad looked delighted with himself, obviously having bypassed the mirror in his excitement to get going.

"What do you think Dex? I'm not going to lie I feel ten years old again in this strip!"

I couldn't burst his bubble and mention that it was his strip and not him that looked ten years old.

He looked more like *ten billion years old!*

"Dad, are you sure this is a good idea? You're not even that into football. I always beat you by a mile when we play in the garden."

"Nonsense, Dex. I go easy on you in the garden. That's all. C'mon son," he lifted up his set of house keys, clearly eager to get going.

Further protests would be futile.

When Dad gets an idea in his head there is no removing it. It's like a scab on your knee after a tumble at training. You've to put up with it and hope it improves soon.

Mum and Mellissa waved us off grinning broadly. I wasn't sure if they were stifling giggles at Dad's outfit.

44

Or simply cheery at the prospect of a boy-free house for the afternoon.

Either way, it wasn't a good sign.

Dad and I soon arrived at the sports centre which was only a five minute walk from our house.

Thankfully Dad wore a grey hooded sweatshirt over his outfit (which at least matched his socks). So I didn't have to worry about meeting anyone I knew en route.

We were the last to arrive at the sports hall at 2.03 pm.

The other 18 people (9 fathers and 9 sons) had already gathered round the allotted coach for the afternoon.

I had been walking deliberately slowly to the sports centre in the hope that we would miss the match altogether. Obviously I am so fit that even my slow walk is too fast.

Our names were checked off the list by the sports centre's coach and referee for the day - *Mitch*.

Mitch warmly welcomed everybody and split us into two teams. He gave out coloured bibs - Dad and I were in the red team. Half the Super Striker's colours. Thank goodness, a good omen at last. The other team were given blue bibs.

I kept my eyes firmly trained to the ground, feeling mortified.

I only looked up when Mitch announced that we should shake hands with the opposing team members before commencing the match.

As we all went through the hand shaking formalities, Mitch gave an enthusiastic pep talk about the match being just for fun. To encourage families to engage in sport. And that it didn't matter whether you won or lost.

All the nonsense adults tell kids before sporting activities. It's perfectly obvious that the goal is to win and if you don't win you lose.

Get used to it people!

It was only when I looked up and was greeted with the familiar evil smirk that I realised that **TB** was on the blue team.

Along with his father, who needless to say was kitted out in the latest Real Madrid strip. He had added a silver sweat band around his head and one around each wrist.

So obviously meant business.

The smirk was clearly a family trait as his dad had exactly the same sneering expression on his face.

When he shook hands with my dad. I heard him utter a derisory, "Cool socks!"

Dad muttered something about sporting prowess transcending fashion which was lost on TB's father, who clearly not very bright.

Mitch said, "Right chaps, it's only a twenty minute match, so don't you worry if you're a bit out of shape." *I'm sure he looked right at Dad.* "On the blow of my whistle we'll kick things off!"

All too quickly, Mitch blew his whistle to commence play.

Oh no, here we go...

Father and Son Match

The match turned out to be surprisingly good fun.

Within minutes I'd scored a goal for the red team - old pro that I am.

Dad and I turned out to be an amazingly good pairing.

Dad managed to tackle pretty well. And won the ball on most occasions.

TB's dad, despite his state-of- the-art strip, was *terrible*.

He kept on losing the ball and the goals just flooded in for the red team.
By half time, the score was 6-1 to our team.
Mitch gave out orange segments at half time.

TB's father took things far too seriously by changing his shirt to a new one.

Surely he couldn't be so unfit that his shirt was sweaty after only ten minutes of football!

In the second half, TB and his dad resorted to dirty tricks befitting of someone with a deadly disease as a name.

They kept sniggering any time Dad got the ball.
They made cheeky remarks under their breath like:

Did your shirt shrink in the wash? Is grey the new "in colour" for football socks? Feeling a bit bloated, are you?

Unfortunately their tactics worked.

Dad kept looking up to hear what they were saying and kept losing the ball in the process.
The score soon became 6-4.
The Blues were catching up.

I couldn't let TB win.

I was so furious with his foul play that I must admit I did perform a bit of a hack on TB. Simply, to try and prise the ball away from his cheeky, cheesy-smelling feet, you understand.

This resulted in penalty being awarded to the Blue Team sadly.

Which, of course, they scored.

Making it 6-5 to us.

With minutes to go.

I was just about to redeem myself and perform a clean pass to Dad. To enable him to score and impress the TB clan. When I noticed that Dad was rather red in the face and clammy-looking.

I assumed he was mad at the treacherous TB duo.

I whispered, "C'mon Dad, just ignore them. They're idiots. We're better than them and they can't stand it. Let's finish this match off in style."

"It's not that Dex. Those two don't bother me a jot. They can't play for toffee. It's the dad's new shirt. It's so shiny that the gym lights are bouncing off it. And it's bringing on one if my migraines!"

I had noticed the room being considerably brighter in the second half.

I looked closely at TB's dad's new silver football shirt.

It was only then that I spotted lots of yellow bicycle reflective tape sewn into the fabric of the already shiny top.

What a mealy-mouthed cheeky little cheat!

"Cheater!" I blurted out. "Your top's got reflective tape sewn into it. It's bringing on one of Dad's migraines!"

Mitch blew the whistle three times.

"For health and safety issues, I'm stopping the match. Complaints about light bouncing off your strip I'm afraid, Mr Bradley. You'll have to step aside I'm sorry to say. There's only a minute to go. Since it's just a friendly match, we'll call it time. Final score - 6-5 to the Reds!"

"It's a travesty!" spluttered Mr Bradley.

He quickly tore off his short and swapped it for the original one that he had worn in the first half.

"There's nothing wrong with my shirt. I want a refund for the final minute of lost football!"

TB's dad stormed off to speak to the poor, unsuspecting girl at reception.

TB scurried after him mumbling, "Told you shouldn't have brought that other shirt, Dad. It was only meant to be a friendly game."

"That's the spirit!" said Mitch patting TB's back as he swept past.

"Good game guys!" Mitch cheerily addressed the rest of us.

"As the little lad just said, it's only meant to be a bit of fun. Some healthy exercise for all the family. Well done to the Reds who were the victors by one goal. But let's have a huge round of applause for everyone that took part!"

Mitch started off an enthusiastic round of clapping. Even with the echo of the applause bouncing around the gym hall, we all heard the gym hall door slam behind the Bradleys.

The remaining 18 players who had taken part fairly and squarely all shook hands and said *good game* to each other. *It had been a surprisingly good game, despite TB's father's attempts to ruin it.*

Thankfully Dad's colour had returned to normal now.

"Good game, Dexy. I think in future I'll be leaving all this running around to you young ones. And the professionals on the pitch of course."

Dad shook hands with Mitch before we left and said, "Thanks for organising today. I've really enjoyed it. Never mind the wee hiccup at the end. It's just a bit of desperation on the part of the young lad's dad. It was great fun never the less!"

The day had, amazingly enough, been brilliant fun.

Admittedly football of any variety is pleasurable to me.

I was a bit disappointed that Dad didn't feel up to a re-run.

I wouldn't have minded another chance to show TB whose family is top at football.

Image Restyling

The day after the eventful father and son football match, I asked Mum to take me to the barbers.

I think deep down I was concerned that Dad's scarily un-cool image might rub off on me.

Let's hope appalling fashion sense is not a genetic defect.

I decided it was time to revamp my style and look even more like Fabio.

(He was surely closer to my genetics as a top sportsman than Dad.)

I already spike up my hair like Fabio does. But I have never asked the hairdresser to copy his style **exactly** before.

Feeling too shy.

Now that I am hoping to see Fabio in real life with Mikey, if we ever win this blasted competition, I've decided to throw caution to the wind and attempt to become his clone.

That way if Fabio catches sight of me in the crowd, he'll instantly recognise me, as his long lost son.

And claim me.

I decided to take my most up-to-date poster of Fabio. The cover shot from *GOAL Magazine* that Mikey kindly gave me to the salon.

Mum seemed a bit embarrassed when I suggested carrying my dog-eared poster of Fabio all the way to the barbers.

I don't know why because I've often seen her rip out photos of TV stars to show to *her* hairdresser.

It's not embarrassing for her to want to copy the look of a famous star now, is it?

The strange thing was the glossy poster I intended to take had disappeared from my bedroom wall!

All that remained, in its pride-of-place position above my bed, was the four pieces of blue tack that I'd used to stick it up with.

Assuming it had fallen down, I pushed my bed out.

I only found, however, a scrunched up Arsenal poster (I supported them when I was in Primary 1), a pencil, some red jelly sweets (I would have been saving them as a treat since red is my favourite football colour) and 3 old football trading cards from the 2008/9 season.

When I told Mum about the missing poster, she didn't seem to realise how serious it was. She casually remarked that it must have slipped down behind the wardrobe next to my bed. Dad would need to help me hunt for it when he got back at the weekend.

"But it's the latest one of Fabio and I want to look exactly as he does *right now!*" I complained.

"You'll need to choose the next most up to date one then, Dex. Melissa's due out of gymnastics at five o'clock. If you don't hurry up, we won't have time for your hair to be cut at all."

Reluctantly, I prised away another poster from my wall.

It was of Fabio clenching his fist.

I hoped the hairdresser would be able to copy his hairstyle exactly: 11 cool spikes, with the sides neatly gelled and 2 to 3 random strands swept in a side fringe across the forehead.

This poster wasn't as close-up as the cover shot unfortunately.

"I'm sure that one will do nicely," said Mum, looking at her watch.

We arrived at the barbers at 4.32 pm.

The hairdresser was called Lexi and had dyed blonde hair with very black roots. Her hair was in a fairly spiky style too but Mum called it *layers*.

Mum whispered something in Lexi's ear and they both smiled. I thought I heard Lexi say, "*Short back and sides - no problem.*"

I wasn't exactly sure what *short back and sides* meant but it didn't sound very cool.

Lexi didn't seem to look at the poster very often. And the style she gave me did not match Fabio's terribly well.

However once the hair gel came out things improved massively. Lexi did a pretty good job of copying Fabio's cool spikes with some fruity-smelling hair putty. I counted 11 spikes in total, the same as Fabio in the poster. So overall, a good result.

Mum paid Lexi £7 for the haircut and left a £1 tip. Lexie offered me a lollypop from the sweetie jar.

I chose a red one, of course. Never too old for a lolly!

We then rushed to collect Melissa from her gymnastics class.

Mel clambered into the car wearing her fancy green and silver gymnastics leotard.

Every inch of her was covered in badges that displayed her ability to contort her body into strange and wonderful positions.

Mel cruelly remarked, in a true sister-like fashion, that I looked nothing like Fabio.

"Like you know anything about footballers," I retorted.

"I see Fabio every time I am unlucky enough to enter your room," replied Melissa. "And I can assure you – you look nothing like him."

"Stop squabbling!" said Mum. "Or there's no TV when we get home."

Football Fun started at 6 pm so I maintained a dignified silence.

I stared down at the poster of Fabio scoring.

It was like looking in the mirror.

What does Melissa know anyway? She has no taste.
*You only have to go into **her** room to see that.*

To pass the time in the car journey, now that fighting with Melissa was out of the question, I turned round the poster of Fabio and read the article printed on the reverse.

Here is what it said -

> *"Football has been proven to benefit a child's life well into adulthood. Expert psychologists have discovered a number of key life lessons that a child learns from playing football, namely:-*
>
> *Teamwork: Children benefit from working as part of a team, co-operating and supporting one another.*
>
> *Discipline: Attending regular training sessions, matches and following coaches' rules, encourages discipline.*
>
> *Goal Setting: Kids work hard to score goals and win matches. League tables help children to aim for the top.*
>
> *High of Success: Footballers talk of the massive high they get from scoring – above all else, football is fun."*

I could not agree more.

I read the article out to Mum and Melissa.

Even though Melissa protested loudly that she was not *remotely* interested in football.

Mum replied, "We'll work as a **team** to sit quietly in the car. Follow my **disciplinary rules** and behave. **Succeed,** and we'll celebrate achieving this **goal.** With some delicious chocolate and fudge ice cream for pudding!"

Way to go Mum!

Never mind Fabio, maybe you should become my new coach with a pep talk like that!

September Research Topic

Football Training Drills

Dribbling - *Keeping possession of the ball requires speed, accuracy and good coordination. At Monday training sessions we dribble the ball around ten cones. If anyone accidentally scuffs a cone, they take the walk of shame back to the beginning to repeat the drill.*

Tackling -. *This skill is vital to ensure the enemy -* **I mean opponent** *– loses the ball without a foul being called. Players should practise blocking moves (rushing out in front of the opponent. Then extending your leg to try and gain the ball). As well as the more tricky poking tackles. This is where you start off behind or at the side of your opponent and extend your leg to try and win the ball.*

Passing - *Practise controlled passes. Practise short, simple passes. As well as longer ones that are harder to control.* **I always pair up with Mikey to practise passing skills at training. Since he and I make such a great team.**

<u>Heading</u> - *Heading is a skill that comes with practise. Aim for 10 shots at heading per training session.* **I will add this to my daily training regime.**

<u>Shooting</u> - *Practise penalty shoot-outs as often as possible. These may be crucial to a match result. Aim for 20 shots per day.* **My current PB at penalties is 18/20 – not too shabby!**

October 2011

"A goal from Fabio in the opening few minutes meant the Strikers led practically all the way..."

October Match Result: Super Strikers v Super Kickers 5 – 3

Overall Result: 3 - 0 to the Strikers

My Results

Goals to date for Eastwood Rovers:

11 - Me and 8 - TB *(Ha, ha to the boy whose family uses dirty tactics at family football matches!)*

New Skill:

Kick the ball in the air with your right heel. Spin around swiftly (to outwit your opponent and put them off-guard). Re-gain the ball on the way down. And score.

Simple!

Training Regime:

In addition to last month's training *(which seems to be working since I am finally Top Scorer)* I've added *(so I don't become complacent)*:-

Heading:

10 headers a day (as suggested by my research into football skills).

Dribbling:

Have placed 8 plant pots in a zig zag across the back garden.
Will practise dribbling around them 10 times a day.
No risk to Mum's pots at all.

This drill lasted two days. When I accidentally knocked over one of Mum's best blue ceramic pots. It then shattered noisily into smithereens.

This was nothing compared to the noise of Mum's screeching. Advising the garden's not a football pitch but an area for family relaxation.

Who wants to relax in a garden when they can practise football out there? Honestly, what planet do mums come from?

Weight lifting:

Am lifting a tin of lentil and bacon soup above my head 30 times a day in my bedroom before bed to increase my upper body strength. *Dad said this was invigorating, rather than sleep-inducing. So I must perform it in the mornings, before breakfast, instead.*

Research Topic: Common Football Injuries.

<u>Super League Update</u>

The Super Strikers got off to a flying start this month.

Fabio scored in the opening three minutes.

A relief after he made us wait until 89 minutes last month.

It was the Super Strikers second high-scoring match of the season. Their top performance redeemed them from last month's disappointing scrape to victory.

The Super Kickers' captain vowed to their misguided fans that his team would *go all out* to notch up their first win next month.

The Kickers have been plagued by injury.

Their top scorer missed the September match due to a hamstring strain. Also one of their best defenders has been out of action for the last *two* matches with a calf muscle injury.

Hopefully the Super Strikers team will remain in tip-top health to see off the Kickers' fired up team next month. I've decided to research common football injuries at the end of this month. I don't want to miss any vital games / training due to a pesky injury that could have been avoided!

Little did I know a whole host of other factors would cause me to miss lots of games this season...

<u>Sharpes Here We Come!</u>

Dad was suitably inspired by our father and son football match.

He decided to go back on the internet and see if he could get hold of any tickets for us to see a live game. To watch how the professionals perform!
He decided to try and get tickets to see the Edinburgh Sharpes, Fabio's team in the Scottish Premier League.

As I said, I'm going to leave all the running around to the professionals, he told me.

Unfortunately these tickets, although not as hard to get hold off as *Super League* ones, are still thin on the ground.
With almost every match selling out.

I had yet to hear back from *GOAL Magazine*. So I pinned all my hopes of ever meeting Fabio on Dad getting hold of an elusive pair of *Sharpes'* tickets.

I pestered Dad (at least once every 10 minutes). As he sat at the computer in our family living room, to see if he'd managed to find any *golden tickets.*
His eyes remained glued to the screen.
When I asked him for approximately the eighteenth time if he had had any success, Dad calmly reminded me that patience was a virtue.
After around three hours of frantic typing, scrolling, studying, and searching, Dad excitedly advised that he had found a site that offered Sharpes' games' tickets.

Dad kindly ordered two tickets for the Sharpes match against Western Wanderers on Saturday 30th October at 3 pm.

So exciting.

I was most impressed with Dad's efforts and perseverance. And gave him a massive bear hug as a reward.
"They don't issue the tickets until the week of the match," Dad reminded me. His brow was all sweaty from the effort of tracking down the tickets. *Hope none of it rubbed off onto me!*

"Can't wait!" I remarked truthfully.

*Patience is not one of **my** virtues, that's for sure.*

Not as amazing as a Super League match ticket. But a very close second indeed.

I was dying to pin the elusive match ticket onto the pin board in my bedroom.
I stuck all my football achievements proudly there.

I ranked getting to see Fabio, as an achievement.

TB's Dirty Tactics

The Rovers played an accomplished match on Saturday 10th October. I thankfully remained a high scorer for my team. And reckon I am well on track for getting Fabio to notice me.
I'll be sure to get my name in all the newspapers if I can bag the top scorer trophy *twice* in a row.

Hopefully not joint with TB this time. Joint seems less impressive somehow...

I found the back of the net no less than SIX times.

Each of them belters if I say so myself!

Thankfully TB had been banned from the match by his mum due to a misdemeanour at school the day before. So I didn't need to see his jealous face.

Here's why TB was banned-

Like his dad at the ill-fated father and son football tournament, TB got himself into a spot of bother at school due to underhand tactics.
*TB really needs to read up on **fair play** if he's serious about a career in sport.*

TB **stole** Mikey's signed photo of Ryan Giggs while we were all playing outside at lunchtime.

He pretended he had forgotten his snack: a chocolate biscuit – *not very healthy for someone aiming to be a top athlete.* And told the classroom assistant that he felt faint. He made out he needed to eat something urgently or he would collapse.

His family are such lying sneaks.

The little squirt rummaged around in Mikey's tray until he got hold of Mikey's prized photo.
Then slipped it into *his* reading book.
Inside *his* tray.

I'm thankful TB does not support Fabio and that my property is safe.

Mikey's mum went mental when she found out that Mikey had lost his Ryan Giggs photo at school.
It's worth a lot of money if sold on-line apparently.
Mrs McMillan rang the headmaster, Mr Daley, and demanded an immediate tray inspection of the whole of Primary 6c.

Mikey's mum is a tall, dark-haired lady with a gravelly voice so deep that you might think she was a man if you couldn't see her whilst she was talking.

Her deep voice coupled with her strong Glasgow accent meant that she sounded so ferocious that all of her requests were inevitably met right away.

Mikey was meek as a mouse in comparison to his mum.

Mrs McMillan advised the head-teacher that the school had failed to ensure the security of its pupil's belongings.

She did not take kindly to Mr Daley pointing out that pupils are regularly reminded to keep all valuables at home.

The up-shot was that in order to keep the good name of Eastwood Primary School out of the local papers, Mr Daley agreed to personally check the tray of each person in the class.

When it came to checking TB's tray, the item that aroused suspicion was in fact the book he had stuffed the photo into:-

A *girl's* book. Called *Sally the Sassy Swimmer.*

Mr Daley lifted up the book and remarked, "That's an unusual choice of reading for a boy, Taylor. Is Sally a heroine of yours?"

TB was no stranger to Mr Daley's office as a result of his bullying ways. I think My Daley probably had a good idea who might be behind the missing football photo.

The whole class burst out laughing.

TB swiped the book straight out of Mr Daley's hand, very disrespectfully.

"Desperate to get back to your reading are you Taylor?" asked Mr Daley with a raised eyebrow. Inducing further sniggers from the class.

However as TB swiped at the book – *instead of asking for it back politely as any boy with manners would do* - the Ryan Giggs photo slipped out of his hiding place and fluttered to the ground.

The class laughter was silenced by the shock of the culprit being revealed.

Mr Daley bent down slowly and picked up the stolen item from the ground then held it aloft between his two index fingers, as if it omitted a bad smell.

TB's face froze. Then transformed into a beetroot red colour.

I don't know what he was most embarrassed about - being caught stealing or owning a **girl's** *book!*

Mr Daley handed the precious photograph back to Mikey.

"I believe this belongs to you, Michael. You can inform your mother that the problem has been resolved."

Mikey nodded, relieved to have his prized possession back.

Mr Daley turned to Taylor and gave him a withering look.

"Right, Mr Bradley. You'll need to pay *another* visit to my office. While we contact your mother. *Yet again*. To advise her of your latest antics. Have you anything to say to Michael, young man?"

"Sorry," was all TB could mumble.

He did indeed look very sorry about the whole situation.

"Apology accepted," replied Mikey nobly.

Although he failed to resist adding, "Were you worried you'd miss a tip on how to swim sassily?"

The class stifled more giggles as poor TB was marched off to Mr Daley's room to have his mum summoned to the school. Again. To discuss the serious issue of her son's unacceptable stealing (and possibly reading) habits.

Needless to say (other than for TB) this escapade was the most fun Primary 6c had had in ages.

Even more than when our teacher accidentally but broke wind three times in a row and we had to open all the windows. So that we could take our fingers off our noses and continue writing out our spelling words.

Except the wind (*outside not inside*) caused all the spelling handouts that were placed on the windowsill to fly all around the classroom...
Causing chaos.
Ace!

TB's mother was NOT impressed with TB's light fingers *causing chaos.*

TB was forced to miss Saturday's game as a punishment.

Dad was glad he didn't need to see TB's dad again, so soon after the tournament.
Dad did remark that TB's dad had got off lightly as the weather was particularly stormy that day.

They are jammy those Bradley chaps!!!

<u>Eastwood Rovers Match</u>

Unfortunately TB was back from his one match ban to attend the Eastwood Rover game on the 17th October at 9 am against Netherlee Athletics.

I decided this would be the perfect opportunity to practise my new footie skill. And frighten TB by how much I had improved in his short absence.

I learnt my new shooting technique by carefully studying a football demonstration on the Super League Website.

The cool manoeuvre involved kicking the ball as high up in the air as you can manage with your heel.

Then whizzing round to throw your opponent off balance. (Whilst retaining your own balance.) And then skilfully catching the ball on its way down. Then popping it in the back of the net, as the grand finale.

Or that's the plan.

I have been diligently practising my new move in the garden with Melissa all week. Mel *hates* football training. She only agrees to help me, so I can become skilled enough to get picked up by the Scottish Football Development Agency. It trains talented youngsters FOUR times a week.

This would leave Mel in peace most nights after school.

We managed the manoeuvre successfully 6 times in total (out of 20 attempts). Before the ball shot over the fence into the neighbour's garden.

The lost ball will join my 3 other misdirected footballs, 6 tennis balls and Melissa's Frisbee.

The neighbours have the patience of the most patient of saints.

Often, I am sitting watching television in our family room only to find it is raining sports apparatus. As the neighbours throw back a shower of balls over the fence!

Now that's the kind of rain we like in Scotland.

<u>Match Summary</u>

The match got off to such a blinding start, that we could never have foreseen the horrific ending...

Mikey kicked off proceedings by scoring a superb goal into the bottom left-hand corner of the net within 12 minutes. As a result of a swift pass from me. And then excellent ball control by Mikey.

All those dribbling drills are obviously paying off for us!

There followed a hat-trick of goals by me.

All within the next 20 minutes.

Eastwood Rovers were on fire.

The score was 4-0, with 5 minutes to go until the half-time whistle.

At this juncture, however, Netherlee stepped up the pace dramatically.

Our goalie saved at least three near-misses by the Netherlee squad. Unfortunately he could not prevent one ball whistling past him.

Still, the comfortable half-time score was 4-1 in our favour.

It was Mum's turn to provide the refreshing orange quarters this week. The mums take turns to provide the half-time refreshments. This meant she stayed and watched the match and supported me.
Luckily Melissa's Saturday morning ballet class wasn't on that day. She has a dress rehearsal on Sunday instead for her up-and-coming dancing show next weekend.

*That will be fun for me to watch – **not!***

This meant the whole family was in the crowd cheering me on.
It was surprising just how much this spurred me on.

In the second half, TB was very frustrated that he was yet to put himself on the score card.

I'm sure he'll be as aware as I am, of my two goal lead in the top scorer stakes.

He performed a dreadful tackle out of desperation to get some ball action. This resulted in a penalty being awarded to Netherlee.

Unbelievably, they missed!

We were all jubilant.

We could see Netherlee's spirits sinking like a stone.

As Netherlee became more tired and disgruntled, *their* tackles became messy.

We were eventually awarded a corner in the second half.

Which Mikey bravely took. He managed a David Beckham-style swooping corner kick straight to the base of my right foot.

Respect.

Not one of the Netherlee defenders could match my speed - *from all that sprint training no doubt* - as I sprinted to the goal.

Goal!

Making it 5-1. At 80 minutes.

Mikey and I celebrated with our usual rubbing each other's cool spiky hair move. We then pulled our t-shirts up over our faces and fell to our knees and began spinning round and round in circles.

I could hear Mum, Dad and Melissa cheering and clapping loudly from the bustling sidelines.

Mikey and I became a little too fired up by our strong allegiance.

We continued chanting, "*Top Team, Top Two!*" and pointing at our good selves. Until eventually the referee had to blow his whistle for so long that all the clapping and cheering from the crowd stopped. I could see Mel put her hands over her ears. Mum and Dad began to look down at the ground as if they were examining their choice of footwear.

I couldn't stop my body buzzing with the excitement of scoring four goals in one match.

It was a *personal best* by a long way.

My ears were still ringing with the sound of the referee's whistle and the crowd's cheering on my next touch of the ball.

I decided to try out my new skill.

And attempt to make the score 6-1.

The Rovers were so far ahead there was nothing to lose.

Unfortunately I think all the adrenaline and noise had affected my balance.

When I raised the heel of my foot, to kick the ball, I wobbled forward.

As I struggled to regain my balance, the back of my other foot accidentally knocked TB in his private parts.

This sent TB flying to the ground, squirming in agony.

As a result of TB's flailing about he caught the ankle of a Netherlee striker. Who immediately lost his balance and decked it.

Personally I think TB was hamming up his injury to take the shine of my victorious day.

It backfired on him however when the referee awarded Netherlee *another* penalty. And TB was sent off for hacking.

This time Netherlee had no problem firing the ball into the back of the net to make it 5-2.

The referee obviously didn't realise what a terrible faker TB was.

Sadly *I* was also shown the red card for *dangerous and unsuitable play*.

The End Result was-

- The final score was 5-6 to Netherlee who lapped up Eastwood Rovers being two (of their best) men down.

- Mum and Dad banned me from playing football in the garden all weekend. They felt it was a dangerous sport and didn't want me injuring precious Melissa like that poor boy, Taylor Bradley.

- Mum and Dad banned me from watching any football on TV all weekend.

- TB whispered in my ear as he stumbled off to find his dad, clutching his you-know-whats, that

it was all my fault. He was going to make sure *he* won top scorer again this year to pay me back.

A sorry end to the month, I'm sure you'll agree.

<u>Disappointing News</u>

The bad news just kept on coming.

On the **29th October** at **6.13pm,** two days before the Sharpes' match that Dad had booked, Dad broke the devastating news to me that we weren't going to be able to go.

I don't know who was more upset - him or me.

Dad has never watched a live football match before. Since he was brought up in a small village in the Scottish Highlands.
He would have loved to have gone along, now I was old enough not to be a pest. Charming.

Dad was the victim of an internet scam.

Dad had paid the enormous sum of £285 on 1st October for two tickets to see the Sharpes match on 30th October from www.getfootballticketscheap.com.

(The tickets were NOT cheap – that's the first fraud.)

The company was meant to send Dad an email a week before the match confirming the tickets had been dispatched. Despite the enormous amount of money Dad had paid. And copious telephone calls from him chasing them. And angry emails from him, berating them. He heard nothing further.

No wonder Dad was so cagey any time I asked to see the tickets for our father and son outing.

It was daylight robbery said Mum.

I asked Dad if TB or TB's Dad could be to blame for the scam.
He laughed and said, "No, Dexy it's a company in London. Don't worry the police are investigating it. We'll get all our money back. Eventually."
The website has been closed down now, apparently.
As have my dreams of seeing Fabio play live.
I HAVE to win this blasted competition.

What in the world is taking them so long to decide on a winner?
Surely it clearly is MY entry.

I worry that my chances of success are looking increasingly unlikely as the days go on.
"Don't worry son," consoled Dad. "Once the police have recovered my funds, I'll go through the official

Sharpes website next time. A lesson learnt and all that, eh, Dex?"

"How long did the police say it would take to get our money back?"

"Up to six months. We'll be needing more of that patience I was talking to you about Dexter." He ruffled my hair as he always does when trying to cheer me up.

I felt tears of disappointment and frustration sting at the back of my eyes. I tried hard to fight them back. I couldn't explain to Dad the double whammy of loss I was experiencing. I was missing my chance to see Fabio play AND meet my new coach and footballing father figure.

Six months was an eternity to wait.

I plodded up the stairs to my bedroom. With a heavy heart, I rubbed out *Dad and Dexter's Football Trip* from the 31st of October on my Fabio Galianto 2011 Calendar.

I must confess a lone tear helped rub away the writing.

October Research Topic

Common Football Injuries

1. Football injuries are usually sustained to the lower parts of the body since its the legs that do all the hard work in football! The most prevalent ones are hamstring sprains, sprained ankles, torn knee cartlidge and hernias. **OUCH!**

2. A third of all football injuries are due to overuse of the muscles, tendons and ligaments that support the body and develop over time. Regular physio is a must to help prevent such injuries and will be provided by the player's Clubs. **I don't know why Melissa is reusing to give my legs a wee rub. It's no different to putting on sun tan cream.**

3. Another main cause of footballers' injuries is the trauma to the body caused by colliding with another player **(as happened to me and TB and the Netherlee chap this month).** Or landing from a jump in an awkward position.

4. Footballer players must receive regular physiotherapy sessions aimed at preventing injuries. As well as to treat any existing injuries. **These sports massages can be quite painful. As they work the muscles so deeply in order to gain as much benefit as possible.**

5. The good news is footballers still get paid while they are injured. This will usually be written into their contracts. This means that while they are injured footballers will be paid a small fortune to lie on the couch watching sport, eating crisps and relaxing – **result! Only joking. Injury is every sportsperson's worst nightmare. As it prevents them playing the sport that they love.**

   Prevention is key. So on with the shin pads this Saturday, Dexy!

November 2011

"By the end of the month Fabio found himself in the disappointing position of being a member of two teams that had hit a rocky patch. The Sharpes lost 3 of their 4 matches in November. Despite Fabio's best efforts to shore up the poorly defended team, the Super Kickers went on to notch up their first win in November. It will not be a good Christmas for Fabio unless his teams step it up a gear."

November Match Result: Super Strikers v Super Kickers 0 – 2

Overall Result: 3 v 1 to the Super Strikers

My Results

Goals to date for Eastwood Rovers: Me – 19, TB – 20 *(uh oh!)*

Missing Fabio Posters: 4 (3 of Fabio, 1 containing whole Strikers team)

Personal Training:-
Keepy Uppies: 30
Press Ups: 40
Laps around garden: 30 circuits

Shooting practice: 25 shots.
5 goes at each corner of the net.

Achieved most success with Top Left, scoring 4/5 on average.
Worst - bottom right corner, achieving only 3/5 penalties on average.

Research Topic: How are top footballers spotted?
Bring it on...

Fabio Commentary

Fabio and I are not having a good spell...

The Sharpes have been on poor form of late. They have lost 3 out of their 4 matches in November. Very disappointing for one of Scotland's top teams.
They have now slipped to third place in their league.
Apparently this is the team's worst monthly performance since 1963.

Fabio was still in decent form but the defence let him down. And the quality of passes was such that he could just not find the back of the net.

It must be very frustrating for him.

The Super League match was very frustrating for *me* with the Super Strikers failing to score.

The Strikers had an embarrassing own goal. When Dixon accidentally kicked the ball into his team's own net amidst a scramble to prevent the Kickers scoring.

Cringe!

The Super Kickers went on to score a further goal of their own, with a stunning header by their captain. The Kickers were jubilant at their 2-0 win.

Their first win of the season.

Overall the Super Strikers have won three matches and the Super Kickers have now won one.

So at least Fabio remains at the top job on the top team.

For now...

Post-Match Tactics

At school on Monday all the boys were chatting about my unfair dismissal from the football pitch on Saturday. Everyone was in agreement that it was all TB's fault and that he was acting when he fell down laboriously and tripped up the other boy.

He should consider a TV role rather than a career in sports if he can't handle a light tap.

TB got so upset with the jibes that he lifted up his blue school polo shirt to reveal his so-called bruise. Honestly you needed a magnifying glass to make out the tiny dot. Even then, I am sure it was a freckle he was trying to pass off as a *bash*. This revealing of his midriff of course only led to further snickering at his expense.

TB has performed so many dirty hand tricks and taunted so many people. That nobody had any sympathy for him.

I updated Mikey that Mum and Dad had banned me from watching the Sharpes match on the TV due to TB's performance. Meaning that I'd missed seeing Fabio's wonderful football skills **twice** over. Once, live **and** once, on the television. He was most sympathetic.

Mikey agreed to come round straight after school to discuss other ways of contacting my beloved Fabio. The matter was becoming urgent.

This lifted my football deprived, Fabio pining, unfairly red-carded spirits somewhat.

After finishing his homework in record time, Mikey arrived at my house, true to his word, at 4.11pm on Monday 7th November *(fast work, mate)*. We decided to put the internet to better use than NOT providing Sharpes tickets to legitimate, paying customers. Instead, we looked up-

Fabio's phone number

85

I personally typed into the search engine...

1. Fabio Galianto telephone number

2. Number to ring Fabio Galianto

3. Edinburgh Sharpes captain phone number

4. How to ring Fabio Galianto captain of Super Strikers

5. How to talk to Fabio Galianto from Sharpes on telephone

6. Mobile contact for Fabio Galianto

Would you believe Google did not supply any results? Thought the internet was useful not useless!

We then tried –

Fabio's address

Mikey tried keying into the search engine...

1. Fabio Galianto home address

2. Contact details for Fabio Galianto of Super Strikers

3. How to live with Fabio Galianto

4. How to tell Fabio Galianto that he should be your coach and companion and should be living with you.

Admittedly we were getting a bit desperate by this point.

We couldn't get over Google failing to provide **any** of the correct information yet again.

We were certain that something must be seriously wrong with the computer.

I yelled to Mum, "Mum! The computer's not working properly again!"

I heard Mum stomping towards the dining room. We keep the family computer there so that Mum and Dad can check what Melissa and I are up to on it.

As she came in, Mum mumbled, "You'll have knocked out the USB cable again Dexter. Practising your free kicks with Melissa's party balloon!"

Mum was covered in flour. Her hair looked prematurely grey from all the white flour on it.

Melissa must be baking again.

When we explained our issue with Google to Mum, she was not best pleased.

"Really, Dexter you're not a baby any more. I'm in the middle of something chocolaty and gooey. And could do without you dragging me away when the computer's working fine! Fabio won't place his contact details on the internet for any Tom, Dick or Harry to pester him. You should try his fan mail address – but another time. C'mon boys get off that computer and into the garden for some fresh air!"

I smiled sweetly to Mum.

"Sorry, it's just I wanted to contact Fabio about a *personal* matter – not send fan mail."

"What personal matter have you got to discuss with a professional footballer?" Mum asked suspiciously.

"Well..." I looked guiltily at Mikey. "... just to see if he wanted to play football with me some time. To help me improve my skills."

"You don't need to improve, honey. You're the top scorer for your team. Just stick in there." Mum encouraged me, loyally. "C'mon, save your *personal* chats for Mikey. Off you go and play. I'll let you know once Melissa's chocolate chip muffins are ready."

We logged off.

Once Mum was safely out of earshot – as I didn't want to risk missing out on a chocolate muffin – I whispered to Mikey, "I didn't want just any Tom, Dick or Harry getting hold of Fabio. Only me - his long lost protégé!"

"Another plan spoiled!" agreed Mikey conspiratorially.

"This man is seriously difficult to get hold off."I agreed.

<u>Stroke of Luck</u>

My fortunes have finally shifted.

It did not matter that I could NOT -
contact Fabio by phone.
or by post.
or by email.
or see him at the live Sharpes match.

Since I WILL have the opportunity to see him IN PERSON finally!

I am the most excited I have ever been in my whole, entire ten years of life!

I feel as though my heart, lungs and stomach lining are going to burst through my body due to over-exuberance.

Mum brought a letter addressed to *Master Dexter Hunter* up to my bedroom for me to open on Friday 25th November at 4.15 pm.

I mentally noted the time of this momentous moment as soon as I spotted that the postmark on the letter was stamped *London*.

I prayed that the letter contained good news and was not a polite knock-back.

Mum and Melissa perched on the end of my red Super League duvet-covered bed. Then eagerly watched me tear the envelope open and fish out my letter.

As I had hoped, it was from *GOAL Magazine*.

I read the letter out to my eagerly awaiting audience...

Dear Dexter Hunter,

Thank you for entering the competition in Issue 214 of GOAL Magazine. I am delighted to inform you that your picture has won first place. The judges especially liked the comical nature of your entry. The creative touch of placing a football-shaped trophy as a hat on Fabio's head, decorated as a Spanish sombrero, was very impressive!

As stated in the magazine, the prize is two VIP tickets to see Super Strikers v Super Kickers play live on 31st January 2012 at Hampden Stadium. Kick-off is at 3.30pm. Please note that one of the ticket-holders must be over 18 years old.

As you know this is a very special season for the Super League and your tickets are for the 100th match. I trust you will have an exciting time and hope that you get the result you are looking for!

Yours Sincerely,

Simon Williams
Editor, GOAL Magazine

"Well done, Dexter!" Mum was beaming. "I never knew you were a great artist. I always thought that was Melissa's forte."

Mel looked even more ecstatic than me.

A whole afternoon in January without me obviously appealed to her.

The opportunity to attend the Super League's **100th game** at Hampden stadium was going to be such an honour.

I was finally going to get the chance to see my future coach and father figure on his home turf.

"I don't remember putting a trophy on Fabio's head as a hat," I told Mum.

"Maybe Mikey did that bit," she suggested.

"Mikey had hoped to go with me if I won. But the letter says one of the ticket holders must be over eighteen."

"The two of you couldn't go off to a rowdy football match by yourselves. Your dad will have to go with you. Mikey will understand. We can invite him to the local theme park another day. To celebrate your joint efforts."

I thought my body would literally rip at the seams with excitement. I expected all my rippling muscles to pop out for all to see.

The only drawback was telling Mikey.

At first Mikey did not understand.

Mikey was super-excited, just like me, when I phoned to tell him the amazing news that I had won...

Just as he started chattering about how much fun the two of us would have, I had to burst his bubble.

I said quietly, "Mikey, there's a hitch. The letter says one of the ticket-holders must be over eighteen. My dad's going to have to take me."

"What?" shrieked Mikey "You've got to be kidding – it was my magazine – I only let you enter because I thought we'd go together."

"It must have been in the rules, Mick. You said you'd read them - didn't you spot that bit? Have you still got the magazine? Go and check. If it's not in there we can call them up and query it. Maybe then we can still go together."

Silence.

Mikey had hung up.

Hopefully he was off to check the competition rules.

He didn't phone back for over an hour.

I was starting to get anxious - I didn't want to fall out with my best mate over this.

When Mikey rang back he said in a small voice, "It was in the rules - in a *really* small print. That's why I took so long - I had to get my magnifying glass out to read it. I should have spotted it really. To be honest, I don't think I'd have entered the competition by myself. I can't draw and I wouldn't have thought of a 3D entry. Mum says good friends should be pleased for one another. She said she'll ask Dad to take *me* to see a Manchester United match one day soon."

"You might be going to see Man U? This is a double result then. We'll both get to see our heroes play live. We've got to celebrate. Mum says we can go to the local theme park together to celebrate. Are you up for that tomorrow?"

"You bettcha," said Mikey, sounding like himself again.

What a relief.

"You'll practically be in touching distance of Fabio, Dex. If those VIP seats are as good as they sound."

Mikey was back on side now.

"Touching distance," I repeated in a semi-trance.

I remained in this state for the best part of a week.

It took that long to get over the shock of finally having the opportunity to meet Fabio. Having the chance to fulfil my season's goal of trying to persuade him to become my coach.

But will all go to plan?

November Research Topic

How Are Top Footballers Spotted?

1. Top Football Clubs used to hold trials or talent days but these are mainly things of the past. Most clubs will watch school teams and local clubs play matches at the weekends to screen for talent.

2. Premier League Clubs usually have Academies or Apprenticeship programmes which train young, talented players. Only a handful of players who get into these schemes, however, will go on to have a career in the sport.

3. A National Football Academy is due to open in Dundee in Scotland by 2016. Where young Scots players *(like me!)* will benefit from expert coaching programmes.

4. Talent scouts look for the right attitude as well as play. They will always meet with the player's family before signing up a child. To make sure the child has the right spirit, focus and dedication to succeed.

5. In general, if you are good enough you will usually be found and snapped up!

<u>Action Plan</u>

- Continue to play my football socks off at all matches and help out ALL team mates (even TB) as much as possible to get myself noticed.

- Consider moving to Dundee in 2016 if not scouted by then.

- Beg ... hope ... plead ... pray ... wish ... dream ... cross all of my fingers and all of my toes ... that I AM good enough and that I AM found.

Preferably, in person, by Fabio!

December 2011

"Luck was not on Fabio's side. As he failed to score at the iconic New Year's Eve Super League match."

December Match Result:
Super Strikers v Super Kickers 0 – 2

Overall Result: 3 v 2 to the Super Strikers *Those blasted Kickers are catching up. It's a close run thing now.*

My Results
Training:
0 (too much snow)

Trip to Hampden Stadium:
Hanging by a thread

Super League-type gifts in my Christmas Stocking:
9

Goals scored for Eastwood Rovers this month:
0 (no matches were played due to snow/Christmas holidays.)

Research Topic:
Top Footballers' Requirements

Fabio Commentary

Super League die-hard fans love the *iconic* New Year's Eve match.

Ever since the very first Super League match *EVER* was played on 31st January 1999, as part of Scotland's Year 2000 celebrations. It has remained THE EVENT of the season.

The celebrity football match was so popular in 1999 that the Scottish Football Association decided to make it a regular monthly fixture. In addition to the weekly Premier League ones.

Unfortunately I think this year Fabio has either:-

(a) eaten too many mince pies,

(b) worn himself out going to too many Christmas parties, or

(c) been distracted thinking about all the fabulous Christmas presents he might receive...

Because he was NOT on his best form sadly.

The Super Kickers won again (by 2 goals to nil).

This is the Striker's second match of the season where they have failed to score!

Not a good end to 2011.

I hope Fabio raises his level of play in January when I go to see him. Fingers crossed that 2012 will be the year that the Super Strikers reign victorious once again.

Preparations

Never mind a *Santa* list.

Ever since I found out that I had won the competition prize, I've been compiling a list of all the key items I need to bring with me to the match of a lifetime.

It's not as if I can pop home to Edinburgh if I forget something. And I don't want to make a fool of myself in front of Fabio.

So far, I've jotted down:

1. Super Strikers beanie woollen hat

2. Super Strikers scarf

3. Super Strikers gloves (woollen, not goalie pair)

4. My red football watch (don't want to be late!)

5. Super League fleece-lined winter coat

6. Football Journal (to record all the live action)

7. Binoculars to see Fabio up close. (To analyse how he gets his spiky hair to look so cool. As well as witness his premier league football skills in high definition, of course.)

I decided to begin popping a few essential items for my trip into my red backpack that I take on holiday with me.

Preparation is crucial our coach tells us all the time.

However, I couldn't find one vital item – my Super League scarf. Essential for a footie match, especially in the depths of winter. Mum said that Melissa had been using it as a skipping rope. And that I should check in her bedroom for it.

I don't really like entering Melissa's room.
It is like stepping into a pink princess' girlie, glittery castle. But Mel was out playing with her pal Amy for the day. So I would need to go into her *palace* if I wanted to retrieve my beloved scarf.

I reluctantly tiptoed into Melissa's room.

I was struck, as usual, by the dreadful pastel pink colour scheme.

A terrible shock after my beautiful, classic red room.

Melissa has a fluffy pink carpet with pink fairy-clad walls.
Yuck!

Her bed-spread, curtains, lamp, pictures and calendar all contain princesses' images.

Eugh, Melissa truly has no taste.

I could, however, see my fabulous red woollen Super League scarf, with its white woollen tassels, flung beneath her bed. I tugged on it. And soon realised that some of its tassels had become tangled in the foot of her bed.
I hauled Melissa's bed out, as best I could, to free my poor scarf... **only to discover my four missing posters!**

Any joy I felt at their discovery was short lived.

Aghast. I discovered they had been cruelly destroyed.

They were completely ruined by gel pen marks scribbled all over them. There was no way I could hang them back up now.

I was furious.

I saw red. (Not literally in the sense of the colour of my scarf.)

The cheek of her stealing my four best pieces of wall art.

Then wilfully defacing them!

How outrageous to cover professional, talented, footballing geniuses in sparkly pink and purple glitter ink.

Well, I'll show her! I thought.

Well I didn't so much think as react...

I grabbed Melissa's boldest gel pens – **green, red and black**. Then scrawled venomously all over the princesses' sneering faces on Melissa's curtains.
I blackened out the football-hating princesses' teeth on Melissa's duvet cover.
And may have added a curly beard on their treacherous chins for good measure.

I then stomped out her room in disgust.

There.

That would show Mel not to mess with Fabio.

Or his team-mates.

Or me.

I'd show these non-sporty princesses who ruled...

<u>On the Bench</u>

Unfortunately, it was clearly **NOT** me who ruled.

When Melissa returned from her play-date at Amy's house, she did not recognise me as the boss at all. Or appreciate my adjustments to her room.

Even more unfortunately, Mum - who came racing up the stairs to find out what Melissa's bloodcurdling screams were all about – definitely did not agree with my reaction to Melissa destroying my precious Fabio posters.

She acted as though *I* was the one in the wrong.

Mum did not think about my side of the story. Even though I told her repeatedly -

- Melissa STOLE my special Fabio posters from my room and RUINED them.

- She spoiled my best poster. The one with the close up of Fabio's hair.

- I'm entitled to defend my hero. *Surely?*

**I felt Mum was swayed by Melissa being so upset
and her measly defence arguments...**

- *Sniffle.* "I was planning to return the Fabio posters,
Mum."

- *Sob.* "The gel pen marks were an accident."

- *Sniffle.* "My beautiful curtains and bed clothes are
now ruined."

- *Sob.* "Bedroom linen is worth a lot more than a
few measly posters."

**Well, the last point was Mum's actually.
Mum also seemed to latch on to a few other critical
facts of her own.
Advising me (in an extremely upset/angry tone):-**

- You're older and should know better!

- Your room looks a better with less posters slapped
all over the walls.

- Football posters come free in comics. Replacement
bedclothes and curtains cost over £100.

- You should never draw on curtains. Especially at
your age. Posters are made out of paper which at
least can be drawn on!

Mum concluded by awarding me the wounding penalties of-

- NO FOOTBALL FOR A MONTH. PLAYING OR WATCHING. *Ouch!!!*

- MUM WILL DISCUSS WITH DAD WHETHER I'M ALLOWED ON THIS FOOTBALL TRIP OF OURS NEXT MONTH. *Aaaarghhh!!!!!*

December therefore proceeded as follows...

Bereft. Grieving the loss of being able to tune in and see my beloved Fabio.

Lost. Desperately missing being able to follow all the latest exciting football action.

Football-less. My beloved Super League football is sorely absent from the garden.

My body is suffering terrible aching withdrawal symptoms. I'm unable to kick it or perform my daily training skills. I hope my muscles are not wasting away!

Friendless. I wish my best mate Mikey could come over after school. Even just for a day, for a friendly kick-about.

I must confess to rummaging around in:-

The shed, garage, messy cupboard, sand pit...
All of Mum's usual hiding places...

In search of my precious ball.

No luck.

I hope it hasn't been binned or given away.

An expensive Super League replica ball like that.

It is very dear to me.

Team-less. Eastwood Rovers have suffered without their top scorer. They have lost their last two matches. Play has now stopped for the Christmas holidays. So we'll have no chance to catch up this year.

I fear my football skills may never catch up to their previous top-scoring status. After this catastrophic lack of training...

<u>Christmas Eve</u>

I think my foot's twitching problem will only cease when Mum lifts this deeply unfair and extreme ban.

Surely it was a minor - not to mention justifiable - act of defence. My football posters were being attacked after all.

I have not played or watched ANY football. AT ALL. For exactly 23 days.

It's all Melissa's fault (see diary entry above).

Unfortunately Mum does not see it that way (see diary entry above).

So I am not allowed to prattle on about this constantly in a whining tone of voice, Mum says.

I can only hope that Dad wants to see the Super League game so much that he insists that I am allowed to go.

Mum says she'll make the final decision in the New Year.

Even the prospect of Christmas Day tomorrow does not lift my sombre mood.

I hope that *Santa* is not a fan of pink princesses. Even though he distributes many to little girls every year. I'm sure he's secretly a Super League fan. Since wears red.

Hopefully he'll be on my side.

Maybe I'll even receive a few extra Christmas pressies to cheer me up.

Christmas Day

My spirits are briefly lifted out of the doldrums to celebrate Christmas Day.

Thankfully my good record over the course of the year must have prevailed. Both Melissa and I were fortunate enough to receive gifts in our stockings. Mel checked this fact at 4.20 am and yelled at the top of her voice that –

Santa's been!!!

I confirmed sight of the gifts at 4.21am.
We both told Mum and Dad – doubly loudly since there were two of us screaming in excited pitches –

There's loads of presents downstairs!!!

Mum and Dad were rather bleary-eyed and incoherent.
Dad mumbled, "That's exciting news. But it's the middle of the night kids. Back to bed. And wait until at least seven before opening your presents."

"Seven!" We wailed as if Dad had suggested waiting three months before opening our eagerly-awaited, beautifully gift-wrapped presents.

Dad just about jumped out of his skin at our screeching.

"Okay – six thirty then. But no earlier," he compromised in order to get back to sleep.

"We'll aim for six." I offered. "Thanks Dad, love you!" I raced out the room before he had a chance to barter further.

I reluctantly returned to bed although getting back to sleep was much trickier.

I was so thrilled by the prospect of receiving all the football-related gifts that I'd requested in my detailed Christmas List. (It ran to three pages.) There was no way my mind could rest. Even if my body wanted to.
When I next checked the clock it was 4.34 am. And then 4.40 am. Luckily at my next glance it was 5.24 am, so I must have got some sleep.

After that I was pretty much awake and counting down the next 36 minutes until unwrapping time.

I checked my Super League digital alarm clock at 5.26, 5.28, 5.29, 5.34, 5.35 – toilet break – 5.45, 5.47.5.50.5.53. 5.54, 5.55 am...

At which time Melissa obviously decided it was near enough to the agreed time. And could be heard jumping up and down on Mum and Dad's bed, yelling, "It's Christmas!"

I raced downstairs to the front living room where our stockings had been carefully laid out the night before. They were literally brimming with presents.

I was closely followed by Melissa.
Then Mum appeared.
Reminding us, as she tugged on her dressing gown, not to open anything until she had her camera ready.

It took me precisely 52 minutes to open all of my gifts. Melissa took a bit longer – 1 hour 24 minutes – to open all of her presents. As she insisted on setting up and playing with her new dolls' house as soon as she opened it.

Christmas was a super-star event, as usual.

My stocking was *stocked up* with all the latest football games, books and clothes that I could dream of. And I do a lot of dreaming about football!
I was lucky enough to receive 9 football gifts, 4 Lego gifts, 8 items of clothing, 2 books, 1 money box, 3 DS games, 2 Xbox games and 3 edible gifts.

My favourite three gifts were:-

1. The Edinburgh Sharps away strip. (I already have the current Super League strip and Sharps home kit.)

2. A Super League bubble gum dispenser with 100 juicy fruity bubble gum balls inside.

3. New football boots (the same as Fabio's).

Melissa also received most of the items on her lengthy wish list.

She was delighted with her 8 princess-style gifts, 10 items of clothing, 4 dolls, 1 Barbie Goes Swimming set (another doll, I suppose you could say), 1 pink Lego kit, 2 horse-play sets, 1 jigsaw (unlucky!), 3 edible gifts and of course the dolls' house that she wanted so badly.

Why she would want to play for hours on end with tiny pieces of furniture and miniature dolls is beyond me.

But at least it gives us all a break from her sing-a-long microphone renditions. They are belted out at an alarming decibel. Even louder than Dad's bellowing snoring. And that's saying something!

Gran arrived at 3.57 pm after watching the Queen's Speech in her own home, which she likes to do. She bore more exciting pressies for us kids.

I received the new Fabio calendar (12 heavenly shots of my hero - perfect) and a football duvet cover set (bringing the total of my football-related gifts to 11).

Melissa got a new princess calendar and t-shirt (bringing her total of princess-related gifts to 10).

After we had opened the rest of our gifts that had been sitting under the tree for weeks, tantalising us, Mum meticulously noted down who got what and from whom. (For the dreaded thank you notes.)

Finally, it was then time for Christmas dinner.

I was looking forward to my Christmas dinner this year. Not because I was hungry. (I had already polished off a bar of milk chocolate, a packet of white chocolate buttons, 10 jelly sweets, 9 chocolate coins and a fudge bar.) But because I had been secretly working on **an after-dinner speech.**

It was the tradition in our house for Dad to give a family version of the Queen's Speech.

I had prepared a poem of my own this year. For the first time ever. To try and redeem myself. And return to Mum and Dad's good books again.

So they will allow me to see the Super league match next month.

Fingers crossed.

Here goes...

Bring on the Speeches...

After the whole family had stuffed themselves with lentil soup to start.

Turkey with all the trimmings for main (naturally).

Chocolate cake for pudding. (Since no-one likes Christmas pudding in our house).

Dad made his little speech.

It contained all the usual stuff. About being grateful for our lovely family. Trying to spend more time together. How he's looking for a job nearer to home. How we should be grateful for all our lovely presents. How Christmas was about more than just getting lots of gifts... he lost me at that bit.

Dad got a good round of applause when he finished.

So the grown-ups must have liked it.

Mum refilled the glasses with champagne for the adults. Apple juice for Melissa. And diet cola for me as a treat for this special occasion. I don't usually drink fizzy drinks as they are too unhealthy for a top athlete like me.

I picked this moment to announce that I had a heart-felt poem to read out.

The room went silent.

Mum and Dad appeared stunned. They stared at each other in quiet confusion.

Gran nervously rustled her purple paper party hat. The one she took it off when her hair got hot and sticky.

Melissa on the other hand looked keen as a bean to hear my speech.

"Good for you, Dexy," slurred Gran, eventually.
The champagne had obviously taken effect.
She placed her scrunched-up party hat back on her head for the occasion.
Gran commanded brightly, "Off you go, lad.
Entertain us with your ditty!"
"Yes, over to you," said Dad who had recovered his composure. He gestured grandly for me to take centre stage.

Melissa put down her toffee centred chocolate in order to listen intently to my efforts.

Here is what I read out-

Santa's suit is white and red.
Just like the Super League cover on my bed.
I think it's a sign that Santa's on my side
Maybe his sleigh will give me a ride.
All the way to Hampden to see Fabio score.
Lovely, kind parents - don't punish me anymore!
I am very sorry for ruining Melissa's princess curtain.
I'll be well-behaved next year - of that you can be certain!

Feedback

It took a little while for the trickle of applause to start.

It was actually Melissa that started it off.

Mum and Dad still looked a bit shocked...

In a good way I hoped. They certainly joined in loudly along with Mel's clapping. As did Gran. Although she did tend to cheer anyone brave enough to read out a cracker joke so was somewhat easily impressed.

"It's really touching that you took the time to write such a lovely personal poem. And learn it off by heart, Dexy," said Mum. "I never knew that Super League match meant so much to you."

"You're a good lad," agreed Dad. "I knew what it meant to you, Son. Don't worry we'll be going - provided you've forgiven your rascal of a brother, Mel?"

Melissa stared stony-faced at me. I held my breath.

"I forgave you ages ago!" said Melissa, breaking into a smile. "I prefer my new curtains anyway." She came over and gave me a great big hug. I think maybe Mum had swapped her apple juice for wine or something. As Melissa NEVER, EVER hugs me.

If I knew that writing a few lines of rhyming words would have this effect on my family I would do it more often. Especially if I wanted something really badly like a dog or something.

I read my poem three more times as everyone kept calling out, "Encore! Encore!"

This was the best Christmas EVER.

I couldn't wait for next year to arrive.

I was desperate to resume normal footie playing, practising and watching.

Mum and Dad lifting the football ban was the best Christmas present I could have hoped for.

I found myself singing my own little rendition of jingle bells with pure happiness radiating from my excited ten-year-old body...

Jingle Bells! Fabio smells!
of sweat from scoring goals.
I can't wait to see his skills
as a VIP- what thrills!

<u>Boxing Day</u>

I was the over the moon to be back in the land of football heaven.

It was even better to enjoy my favourite sport with Dad, who was home for every day of the two weeks of school holidays.

We were glued to the Boxing Day action.

The Sharpes won their match 3-0. But the Super Strikers shockingly lost their Hogmanay match.

So it was not a fabulous end to the year for Fabio.

Let's hope his form improves in the New Year. When I'll finally manage to set eyes on my future coach, lifelong companion and father-figure (no offence, Dad!).

Assuming there are no further setbacks...

December Research Topic

Top Footballers' Requirements

1.   <u>Speed</u> - of feet AND reactions (YES)

2.   <u>Ball control</u> (GOT, I hope) Managers can determine from as young as 12 years old whether the quality of a child's ball skills is such that they are technically gifted. As opposed to just a good player. The majority of kids scouted do not go on to have a future in the game. Only a few are skilled enough.

3.   <u>Ability to score</u> (except Goalie/defender) (TICK)

4.   <u>Accurate passing</u> (OH YEAH)

5.   <u>Stamina and fitness</u> (SURE – *see monthly training regime*)

6.   <u>Love of the game</u> (YES – *in bucket-loads*)

7.   <u>Dedicated playing and practising as a youth</u> (SURE)

8. <u>Competitive spirit</u> (TICK)

9. <u>Thinking BEFORE feet touch the ball</u> (CERTAINLY)

10. <u>Teamwork</u> (OF COURSE – *except if Taylor Bradley is present*)

<u>Overall Result</u>
I dfinitely meet all the requirements of a top footballer.

Come and find me, talent scouts!

January 2012

No quote from the Super League Bulletin about Fabio.

I WAS AT THE MATCH!!!

Simply read on, for MY personal view...

My Results

Super League Matches at Hampden Stadium Attended: 1

Chances of Returning:
0

Goals Scored (prior to trip):
7 - Me, 7 – TB

Totals now are Me - 26, TB – 27
(Drat!)

Research:

What Makes A Good Coach?

<u>MATCH OF MY LIFE</u>

Super Strikers v Super Kickers
31st January 2012
Kick Off - 3.30pm
Venue – Hampden Stadium, Glasgow

After 30 torturously long days and nights – I wish I had a chocolate advent calendar to ease the pain of counting down those days down – the day had finally arrived.

Match Day.

It was even more difficult to sleep the night before Match Day than on Christmas Eve.

And that is saying something.

In the early hours of the 31st of January, I woke at 3.11am.

And then failed to return to sleep at all...

I had to wait in bed with my body pulsating with excitement. Until dashing through to see Dad at the pre-agreed time of seven o'clock.

That's 3 hours and 49 minutes of clock-watching.

I would run out of paper if I attempted to note down all the times that I checked my clock that day!

Dad and I got a lift to the stadium from Mum. We arrived at one o'clock in plenty time for the half three kick off. So Dad and I had bags of time for a bite to eat to make it a special day out.

As if that was in any doubt!

Mum looked quite emotional when she said goodbye to me. And showered me with hugs. As if I was off to war. Rather than my first ever Super League match.

It was a beautiful day.
Unusually for Scotland there was no rain.
The sky was a clear, piercing blue, without any clouds. It was rather chilly. I was glad of my Super Striker hat and scarf to keep me warm.
Dad, for some reason was not that keen on me wearing them until we got to Hampden Stadium. Not

everyone in Glasgow is a Super Striker fan you know, he worried. But it was so cold that I refused to take them off. So Dad suggested hurrying to find a restaurant for lunch which would be nice and toasty warm. I had been so excited that I hadn't eaten anything all day – not even breakfast.

There were loads of cool restaurants and cafes to choose from. But as soon as I spotted a pizza chain that I knew, I asked Dad if we could go there. I loved getting dough balls, followed by an adult-sized pepperoni pizza.

None of this kids' menu, tiny portions malarkey for a growing boy like me.

Thankfully Dad agreed and we heated up nicely over lunch. We chatted enthusiastically about what the score might be today. 2-1 to the Strikers, we decided.

Pudding was ice cream with toffee fudge sauce.

Dad wouldn't allow me a second helping as it was 2.30 pm and the match would be starting in an hour.

My stomach lurched with excitement and I was glad I hadn't eaten that second bowl of ice cream.

Being sick down my Super Strikers outfit would not have been a good look!

Hampden Stadium

Hampden Stadium was like a heaven-sent second home.

It was so familiar and filled with everything I held dear.

The stadium grounds were much bigger and noisier than I had expected them to be.
A sea of Super League fans made their way raucously through the turnstile gates, along with Dad and me.
Some overexcited fans (like I felt) were already chanting songs and cheering on the Super Strikers. Announcing loudly that they would be victorious today.
I considered joining in the frivolity by chanting, "Fabio! Dadio! You really are the bestio!" but I didn't want to upset my real dad.
Especially since he had just bought me an extremely tasty pizza and ice cream sundae.
Dad and I felt very grand and special. As we made our way to the VIP section, to take up our winner's cool vantage point.

Our seats were A25 and A26 – front row!!!

We couldn't have had a better view of the pitch.
We were practically on top of the linesmen.
There were TV cameras and security men everywhere. Carefully guarding the lush, green playing

field. About to be filled with all the top football legends. Including my coach-to-be, Fabio, of course.

I wished that one of the TV camera-men would turn their camera round to face me. So that I could wave at Mikey, Mum, Melissa, Gran and anyone else that knew me.

There were a large number of the other side's fans on the opposite side of the stadium. Ready to cheer on the losing team. But I decided to focus on the match.

It was about to start...

<u>The Match</u>

The atmosphere in the stadium was buzzing.

Everyone eagerly waiting for play to commence and the sporting spectacle to begin.

Every single seat was taken. Certainly there were no spare seats in the VIP section, sorry Mikey!

There was a collective roar as the Super League mascots came onto the pitch at 3.15 pm. Two giant furry chipmunks appeared: one dressed in the Super Strikers outfit and the other dressed in the red and black Super Kickers' version.

They were accompanied by the Chipmunk Cheerleaders who performed a fast and furious procession of kicks, flicks, jumps, twists and turns.

The dads seemed to enjoy it very much.

I politely clapped when they were finished. Thinking that I wished I'd asked for a furry Super Striker mascot toy for my Christmas. Oh well, there's always my birthday in July. I'd just have to wait.

Once the Chipmunks and Cheerleaders had finished their energetic performances and the cheers from the crowd were beginning to die down, a further roar erupted.

The players strode purposefully out of the tunnel and onto the pitch. Hand in hand with the lucky-duck kids that got to accompany them prior to kick off.

I wanted to rip the hand of the angelic little boy with the blond hair away from Fabio. And shout, "Hands off, he's my hero!"

Thankfully the children didn't stay long on the pitch and soon made their way off. I was left to admire Fabio in peace.

I thought he glanced over at me. So I shouted, "Hi Daddio you look awesome. Good luck with the match!"

"What's that son?" Dad asked. "Why are you shouting?"

"Sorry Dad. I was yelling at Fabio. Just some words of encouragement," I muttered.

"Well don't yell next time - you nearly burst my eardrums!"

Never mind bursting Dad's eardrums.

What a noise came from the stadium when the referee blew his whistle.

The match that all the fans had been waiting on for a month (or in my case, a lifetime) commenced.

It was overwhelming.

The game had begun...

The Game

The Super Strikers got off to a flying start.
Within the space of ten minutes, at least five of my favourite players ran straight past me. They performed the most amazing array of passes, crosses, turns and tackles. I'm sure they were showing off their amazing skills directly to me. Since I was seated in the front row of the VIP section and would have looked like a football expert.

I felt so privileged to be able to watch the professional players at the top of their game from such a close vantage point - especially Fabio. I couldn't help but notice how alike we were. I jotted down in my Journal all the similarities between me and the Super Strikers playing at Hampden today.

I wrote-

1. **Accurate passing**
2. **Fast pace**
3. **Good teamwork**
4. **Skilful corners**
5. **Good retention of ball**
6. **Clean tackles**

7.   **Fantastic headers**
8.   **Cool spiky hair**

Every time Fabio whizzed past me I wanted to ask him if he had heard of me yet ... the schoolboy football legend from Edinburgh ... if he might be interested in coaching me ... and becoming my friend ... and father-figure ... and guiding ME so that I become a top footballer like him ... and play in exciting Super League matches like today.

The first goal of the match came from Wilson (via Fabio). Fabio performed a clean pass to Wilson who managed to score from *way* out. It was of the best headers I'd ever seen in my life.

The angle he achieved was just breathtaking.

The score was 1-0 to the Strikers by 4.13 pm.

Thankfully the Super Strikers retained their one nil lead all the way to half-time.

Dad and I were freezing. Despite wearing a vest (on my part), 2 pairs of socks (each) and our Super League hats and gloves.

Admittedly the scarves were off for most of the first half to cheer on our team.

At the half-time break I wrapped my scarf as tightly round my neck as I could manage whilst still being able to converse at great speed with Dad about the exciting first half.

Dad and I munched on our delicious steamy hot pies from the takeaway stand and analysed the game in great detail. We felt like sporting specialists from our front row seat positions.

Dad concluded. "Your man from all your posters – Fabio – he set up some beautiful passes. Especially to his right hand man, Wilson. Didn't you think, Dexy?" asked Dad.

"I couldn't take my eyes off him," I replied earnestly.

"We've got amazing seats. Practically on the pitch with the players!" joked Dad.

"I wish! It's so noisy though, isn't it?"

I've never been keen on too much loud noise. It makes me feel a bit rattled.

"I think all the noise it coming from you, Dexy boy." Dad nudged me in the ribs. "You know you're meant to chant the name of your team or favourite player – not the person who brought you to the match."

How embarrassing.

I must have been calling Fabio "Dad" again in earshot of my other dad. *Life is confusing.*

"I'm just getting carried away with all the excitement." I blushed.

The second half was downhill all the way.

<u>Carried Away</u>

The Super Kickers scored two goals in quick succession putting us 2-1 **down** at 75 minutes.

Fabio had a few chances. He performed an excellent corner pass to Ramsey who hit the post. Just missing out on pulling the team back to a 2-2 tie. At 79 minutes, Wilson was taken off and a substitute was brought on.

As Wilson walked off the pitch towards the bench amid much cheering and applause for his performance, I began to panic that Fabio would be taken off. And I'd never get the chance to see him again. And he'd never get the chance to discover ME. And find out that I want him to be my coach. And friend. And mentor. And second dad – one that lives with us every day.

I decided to seize the opportunity.

At 81 minutes precisely (on my red digital Super League watch that I got for Christmas) I decided it was high time that I said "hi" to my idol. I knew the people from *GOAL Magazine* must have kindly seated me in the front row of the VIP spectator section so that it would be easy for me to pop over the barrier and greet the players.

I could feel Dad tug at the strap of my Super League brick red backpack to try and prevent me from getting away from him and over the barrier. But it was too late. I'd already hoisted my right leg over the metal barrier and jumped down onto the technical area surrounding the pitch where all the linesmen were.

I yelled out, "Hi Fabio! Dadio! It's me, Dexter," at the top of my voice.

It was so noisy in the stadium that neither Fabio nor any of the other players seemed to hear me. I was waving my arms about like a maniac trying to attract Fabio's attention.

It was all to no avail.

No superstar player even noticed me – they were too bust keeping their eye on the ball.

I decided there was nothing else I could do but invade the pitch.

Unfortunately, I only succeeded in placing one toe on the famous green pitch of Hampden Stadium when a rather large, angry looking man in a bright neon yellow jacket marked SECURITY grabbed me an prevented me from placing any further body part on the pitch.

"What do you think you're doing, sonny?" he demanded.

"I'm trying to speak to Fabio. He's my Dad, you understand?" The Large Yellow Security Man looked like he did NOT understand. I faltered, "Kind of. Maybe like a second dad. Hopefully. Soon."

"I think not." Large Yellow Security Man replied with a sarcastic look. "You certainly don't look very Spanish to me. Bit on the pale side. "

I was so annoyed that Large Yellow Security Man was preventing me from getting onto the pitch that I struggled and strained to be free of him. Still calling out all the time to Fabio.

Large Yellow Security Man seemed to find the whole thing rather amusing.

Unfortunately the same couldn't be said for my dad.

Dad had, by now, hot-footed it over the security barrier to retrieve me from Large Yellow Security Man and prevent him sending me to jail for a public disorder offence.

(He told me later amid much ranting.)

"Dexter, get back to your seat immediately, you fool. What on earth do you think you're doing?" Dad barked at me. His face bright red either with fury. Or the exertion of clambering over the high barrier in his less than peak condition.

"Now that sounds like a Scottish accent to me!" said the security guard. "This is your son, I take it?"

"Yes, Sir. Sorry for this inconvenience. It's my son's first ever Super League match. And he's rather excited. He won VIP tickets from a magazine. Many apologies." Dad looked mortified.

"No harm done," relented the guard. "At least he wasn't planning to take all his clothes off and go streaking! Now that would have put the players off!"

Put the players off! The thought hadn't even occurred to me. I would never want to jeopardize a key game for the Super Strikers like that.

"Very sorry," repeated Dad as he thrust me back over the barrier. His face set in stone, clearly furious.

Thank goodness the TV cameras remained trained on the live game the whole time.

I was relieved Mikey and the rest of my classmates – TB in particular – would not witness my humiliation at being manhandled by a security guard.

They would surely all have been watching the game avidly.

"You've made a fool of us," hissed Dad as he grabbed me by the arm and frogmarched me out of the VIP area.

"But, Dad," I gasped, devastated to be dragged away from the VIP area of my beloved stadium. "The match hasn't finished yet. We're going to miss the end."

"We certainly are. Home. Now!" ordered Dad, leading me straight to the nearest exit sign.

I felt tears of frustration and disappointment sting behind my eyes.

I knew this was probably my one and only chance to see Fabio and meet my hero and I'd messed it all up.

"I feel as though I already am home here," I muttered sadly.

As we left Scotland's national stadium, I turned back and watched it fade into the distance. Along with my hopes of ever meeting Fabio...

I'm too depressed to carry out my research into top coaches this month. Feel like my chances of having Fabio ever be my coach have evaporated.

February 2012

"The fans were in raptures as the Strikers held onto their lead in the title race. By their fingertips. Fabio's back in the running to be named the Super League Star Player."

February Match Result:
Super Strikers v Super Kickers 3–0

Overall Result: 5-2 to the Strikers

My Results

Public humiliation: 1

Conversations with Fabio: 0

Conversations with Dad: 100 (or so it seem... *all about my behaviour at the match*)

Only training: Press ups. 30 a day. (I've been spending a lot of time in my room.)

Press Visits: 1

Goals to Date: Me – 34, TB – 30 (yeah!!!)

Research Topic: What makes a Top Coach?

(Will definitely pull my Super League socks up and do my football research this month.)

Super League/Eastwood Rovers Commentary

Unknown.

I have been subjected to a complete football blackout.
I am not allowed to watch any football on the TV.
Attend any football training. Or play any football matches.
Even playing football in my back garden is banned.

All due to *The Incident* at the Super League match.

Reactions to The Incident

The reactions to my attempt to invade the pitch at Hampden Stadium and greet Fabio have been somewhat mixed. **The general thrust of my friends and family's reactions have been...**

Dad: Furious; never taking me to another football match as long as he lives; completely embarrassed; at my age I should have known better.

Overall: Very Bad Reaction.

Mum: I'm too old for such behaviour; what a waste of a lovely seat at a famous football match, with all those hunky footballers playing their hearts out; upsetting my poor Dad like that, when he'd been so looking forward to the father and son outing.

Overall: Quite Bad Reaction.

Melissa: Delighted that I'm banned from football again which means that she can play with all *her* toys in the garden and watch all *her* programmes on the TV i.e. ones for babies/girls.

Overall: Unfair Reaction.

Mikey: Hilarious; good for me having a go at getting onto the pitch; what a hero; what a shame Fabio never came over to speak to me.

Overall: Excellent Reaction.

But there was also a **Surprise Reaction...**

<u>Surprise Visitor</u>

After school on Monday, two days after the ill-fated match, a female newspaper reporter knocked on our front door. She requested an interview with **me.** Regarding *The Incident* at Saturday's Super League match.

Mum was just about to slam the door in the pretty lady's face when the reporter hurriedly assured us that she was not working for the national press. But the **Super League Bulletin** (which I buy every week – that's where the quotes at the start of each month's diary entry come from).

The reporter showed Mum a plastic-covered name badge.

It revealed that she was called Muriel Andrews. The name-badge included a lovely picture of Muriel as well.

She was not smiling in the photograph which made her look rather serious. Even with all her blonde curly hair. But she still looked very attractive. *Mum gets annoyed if I don't smile nicely when photos are being taken.*

Mum inspected Muriel's identification badge very carefully before reluctantly agreeing to let her come in. She led her to our front living room, which is our posh one.

I was delighted to be allowed in the Posh Room. Since this is normally reserved for Mum and Dad's friends only.

Melissa and I (and our pals) have to play in the family room. At the back of the house, off the kitchen. Where all our toys are kept.

The family room is quite handy though because (1) it has no leather sofas that Mum tells me are impossible to remove marks from without damaging the fabric, (2) has no cream carpets for us to destroy as Dad puts it, (3) has no glass coffee table for us to shatter into smithereens with all our larking about and (4) it's right next to the kitchen, which is handy for grabbing snacks and drinks after all our exercise.

It was an honour to pay a rare visit to the Posh Room.

I sank into Mum's comfy cream leather sofa. Whilst Muriel sat politely on the chair opposite me and beamed a beautiful smile straight at me.

Muriel was wearing a long forest green coat over a lime green trousers and matching shirt.

She wore bright red lipstick.

Her golden blonde hair was very shiny and curly.

I thought she looked more like a glamorous film star than a magazine reporter.

Mum announced that she was off to make a nice cup of tea for Muriel. She only took milk in her tea, no sugar. *Very healthy.*

When Mum left the room, I asked Muriel if I could have a look at her fancy name badge. The one that she had shown Mum earlier.

She smiled as she passed it to me and said, "Of course, Dexter. You are Dexter, I presume?"

"Certainly am," I replied, proud she knew of me.

I was very impressed to see the Super League logo on the top right-hand corner of the badge.

Muriel was a fellow fan obviously.

Even without a smile, it was a lovely photo of Muriel who had tied her blonde curls back into a fancy bun on the top of her head.

The badge identified her as: Muriel Andrews, Senior Reporter, Super League Bulletin.

"Very impressive," I said to her, feeling shy all of a sudden and quite glad when Mum returned with the tea tray.

Mum had brought Muriel's tea in a fancy cup and saucer. (Not a mug like she usually uses).

She included a similar fancy cup and saucer containing coffee for herself and an apple juice for me.

There was also three different varieties of biscuits on a fancy cream and gold plate that I had never seen before. I took one of each type of biscuit and munched on them as quietly as possible. Trying to make as few crumbs as I could manage.

Muriel politely declined a biscuit (obviously concerned with retaining her healthy physique). She explained that she had worked for the Super League Bulletin for the past three years.

She told us that to help her complete the magazine columns, she helpfully receives details of any key incidents that occur at any Super League games from the security team.

Muriel pulled out a black patent leather notebook from her fancy green crocodile-skin handbag.

She read out the following notification:-

"At the Super League match on 31st January 2012, the winner of GOAL Magazine's VIP ticket for seat A25, Dexter Hunter, became so over-whelmed with appreciation of Fabio Galianto. That he left seat A25 and propelled himself over the security barrier in an attempt to invade the pitch and greet Fabio. Mark Robertson from the security team detained him until his father collected him. No harm was done. Play remained unaffected."

"Exactly, Muriel" I squealed. "That's exactly what happened!"

I was overwhelmed with appreciation!

I hadn't really thought of it that way – and Dad certainly did not see it that way. But that is the perfect description of events.

Finally an **Understanding Reaction**, from a fellow superfan.

Interview

"Good, well in that case I was hoping to chat with you, Dexter, about the event. So that I can run a feature on you in our Superfans section at the back of the Bulletin," replied Muriel.

I beamed with delight.

The look of relief on Mum's face: I wasn't in trouble after all. I wasn't going to heap shame onto the Hunter family's good name. I was going to be interviewed as a bona fide superfan.

"If that's okay with you, Mrs Hunter?" Muriel courteously sought Mum's approval.

"Of course. Dex is indeed a little over enthusiastic about his football. A great deal of the time. Superfan is a *very* accurate description."

I couldn't believe I was going to see my name in print. In an official Super League Bulletin, no less. Fame at last!

Muriel began to read out some straight-forward questions that she had already prepared in her glittery black notebook. Then carefully wrote down the answers that I gave to her.

In addition, she recorded my replies using a silver hand-held tape recorder.

Muriel explained that this was so that when she got back to her desk at her office she would be able to remember everything I had said. And she wouldn't misquote me!

I told her the device sounded cool and asked for a shot.

But Mum said we didn't have time to play around with it.

The interview proceeded as follows:-

Muriel: So, Dexter, how long have you been a fan of the Super League?

Me (without hesitation): All my life.

Mum (chipped in): Since he was about five years old.

Me: Way before that Mum, remember you and Dad said I came out the womb as a Super League supporter!

Muriel (pre-empting any family disagreements): Okay guys, we'll say as long as you can remember and at least since you were five.

Mum and I nodded in agreement.

Muriel: Have you attended any Super League football matches before?

Me: No, I try every year to order tickets as soon as they go on sale. But I've always missed out. Dad tried to get tickets for the October match. But internet thieves took loads of our money. Then failed to send us **any** tickets.

Muriel: That's disgraceful - you've got to be so careful where you buy tickets these days, with all the internet scams about. I bet you were disappointed. Hopefully the police will track down these rogue traders. It's terrible how they sell fake tickets online. And let down loyal fans like yourself. So, tell me, how did you manage to attend the Super League game last Saturday - you won a competition I believe?

Me: Yes. My best friend Mikey McMillan kindly told me about a drawing competition in *GOAL Magazine*. You had to draw your favourite footballer whilst on his holidays. So I drew a snazzy 3D picture of Fabio Galianto scoring a goal. Whilst enjoying his summer holidays in Scotland, no less!

Muriel (beaming her red lipstick slathered smile at me): Wow, I'm very impressed. I bet not many others drew famous footballers holidaying in sunny Scotland! So you support Fabio? He's my favourite too. You must have been thrilled to win the prize. How was your experience of being a VIP visitor to the Scottish National Stadium at Hampden?

Me: I absolutely loved it! The stadium was so noisy. And I've never seen so much red in all my life! There were red and white or red and black hats, scarves and strips everywhere. It was fabulous. Red's my favourite colour. Like your lipstick!

Muriel (laughing): You'll have been pleased with the score too if you're a Fabio fan – it was 1-3 to the Super Strikers wasn't it? The Strikers are on top form this season.

Me: Yes but unfortunately, I never got to see the end of the match.

Muriel: So I gather. Why don't you tell me why you left the VIP seating area, which had, after all a perfect view of the action?

Me (blushing and in a quiet voice): I wanted to meet Fabio.

Muriel (laughing loudly, again): Didn't you think he was a bit busy at that time, Dexter. Right in the middle of playing an important Super League match?

Me: I was worried he'd be substituted just like Wilson, who was taken off at 72 minutes. Then my chance to see Fabio in the flesh would be gone.

I decided not to mention the whole "dad-thing." Since Mum was sitting opposite me, looking so proud.
Also the article was going to be printed in a Bulletin for everyone to read. And I didn't want my real dad to have to read it and feel upset again. Like when he found out about my letter to Fabio!

Muriel: Oh, Dexter, that's so sweet. I'm sure Fabio would love to meet you too! What is it about Fabio that makes you support him so much over all the other talented players? Is it because he's the captain?

Me: I just feel that we're so alike...

Muriel and Mum chortled.

Me: I mean – we're both top scorers for our teams. I've already scored 28 goals for Eastwood Rovers so far this season you know.

They nodded appreciatively now.

Muriel: That's very impressive, Dexter.

Me: We both have cool spiky hair, both love football...

Muriel: Well, you certainly sound like a true fan to me, Dexter! Last question. We always ask our True Fan to list their three favourite things about the Super League. What would you say yours are, Dexter?

Me: Easy – Fabio's goals, the cool strip and Fabio's hair.

Muriel laughed, sweetly again.

(She seemed to find everything I said funny.)

"That was a great interview, Dexter," Muriel encouraged.

"Quite the little showman, aren't you? So amusing. Well done."

Muriel purposefully clicked off her tape recorder. She then slipped her pen back in its holder inside her fancy leather notebook.

Wouldn't mind one of those myself for my Journal.

"Well, Dexter, it's been a pleasure to meet you. I'm sure Fabio will be delighted when he hears what a loyal fan he has."

"I think I'm a bit more than a fan!" I advised cryptically.

"I'm sure you are," agreed Muriel, pulling on her thick green woollen coat. And placing her notebook back in her crocodile-style bag.

"Will my article feature in GOAL or any other magazine too?" I ask hopefully.

"I'm afraid I only work for the Super League Bulletin. We're not connected to any other magazines. I'm sure you'll be in those magazines one day though Dexter. When you're a famous footballer - right?"

"Cool," I replied. "I hope so!"

Muriel thanked Mum for her time and the cup of tea. She then told us, helpfully, that she'd send us a copy of her article as soon as it was all typed up. She then waved goodbye with a big smile and left to set to work on her vitally important article.

I felt quite sad when Muriel was gone. I liked talking to her about football.

"Well done, Dex," said Mum giving me a hug. "Dad's going to be so proud of you being named the Super League's top fan this month. It's really exciting!"

Mum went off and phoned, emailed, texted, tweeted and contacted on Facebook everyone she knew to say her son was being featured in a famous football magazine.

I only called Mikey. He was super excited. Especially when I told him that I'd informed Muriel that it was *his* magazine that set the whole thing off.

"We're both going to be famous now!" he said.

I hoped Muriel remembered to mention Mikey in her article.

Hopefully Fabio will get a chance to read Muriel's article once it is printed. I wondered if the players get copies of the monthly bulletin sent to them automatically.

I should have asked Muriel.

Never mind.

I'm sure someone as smart as Muriel will be mega-efficient at typing.

So she can send me my copy of the article SUPER-FAST like Fabio's passes!

February Research Topic

What Makes a Good Coach?

Good players require talent but they also need top coaches. (I hope you're reading this Fabio. I need you!).

Important coaching skills –

1. **Enthusiasm** – Children respond well to positive encouragement and praise. This has been proven to work a lot better than shouting and criticising to motivate children and get the best out of them. ***Take note Mum when you are yelling at me for some unintentional misdemeanour!***

2. **Variety** – It is important to make training sessions fun so that the children do not lose focus and get bored. ***No chance of that. I love playing football and could play all day and all night and never get bored.***

3. **Demonstrate the skills** – It's better to be able to demonstrate a skill rather than just talking about it. So that children can actually see how it is done. ***This would be no***

problem to Fabio who could show us exactly how it's done. We'd be trophy winners for sure!

4. **Communication** – Use positive, relaxed body language when dealing with children. As well as speaking to them in a pleasant manner to make them relaxed and able to learn.

5. **Set an Example** – Be a good role model and gain the children's trust and respect. This will set a good example and encourage a good team atmosphere.

6. **Coaching qualifications** – The Scottish Football Association and English Football Association offer coaching qualifications to enable a person to become a qualified football coach.

So come on, Fabio, you know you want to...

March 2012

"Fabio is now the bookie's favourite to be named Super League Star Player of the Year."

Match Results: Super Strikers v Super Kickers 2-2 (both goals scored by Fabio)

Overall Result: 6-2 to the Strikers.

There are only 2 games left this season so the Strikers have it in the bag now. It's now down to the individual players to try and impress the fans to win the medal and prize money for being Star Player.

My Results

Magazine Articles Published: 1

Contact with Fabio: 1

Goals scored for Eastwood Rovers:

12 this month.
A PB.

Must have been inspired by the Top Fan article which also named me as a Future Star Player...

Fame At Last

It did not take long for Muriel to send me my copy of the Super League Bulletin.

I knew she'd be super duper quick on her fingers.

I'm delighted to report that I will now receive free copies of the monthly Bulletin for the next 12 months. Since I'm now officially a Top Fan.

Result!

A large brown envelope addressed to *Master Dexter Hunter* arrived precisely eleven days after Muriel visited for the interview.

I ripped it open as soon as Mum gave it to me.

I flicked right to the back of the magazine. To read my True Fan featured article.

Muriel had made a lovely job of typing up our interview. The only embarrassing thing was that she had included a copy of my latest school photo.

Mum later admitted to sending it to her.

Cringe! *Oh well, at least Fabio would know what I looked like now.*

I was deeply engrossed in reading the detailed article. Then proudly passed it on to Mum and Dad to look at. (It arrived on a Saturday which is very handy since Dad was there for my moment of glory.) So it was Melissa who spotted the hand-written note enclosed with my copy of the article. Assuming it was just a covering note from Muriel, I didn't bother reading it right away. Again it was nosy little Melissa who innocently enquired, "Why has Fabio Galianto written to you, Dex?"

"Fabio?" I screeched, snatching the sheet of paper from Melissa's hand.

My fingers trembled with shock and excitement. I had finally received contact from my hero!

I read his letter to an equally surprised Mum and Dad:

Dear Dexter,

Muriel Anderson from the Super League Bulletin has told me all about your recent VIP visit to Hampden stadium. She said that you tried to invade the pitch to meet me. How flattering! You certainly sound like a true fan to me.

As part of my work with the Scottish Football Development Agency, I go and meet with talented young football players. I am delighted to advise that I am scheduled to come along and meet with you and watch your football training session this Monday (March 12th) at 6pm at your school's playing fields. I'm a bit busy on Saturdays to watch your actual match, as you've probably gathered!

I'd like to repay all your loyal support with some support of my own. Can't wait to see these top football skills that Muriel tells me you have in abundance!

I'm really looking forward to meeting you.

Kindest Regards.

From,

Fabio Galianto

<u>Highlight</u>

This is even better than going to see a live Super League match.

I'm going to meet an actual, alive, real, fabulous Super League player.

Thank goodness for the Scottish Football Development Agency.

I've always hoped they would become involved in my career. They have talent scouts that keep an eye out for raw talent all over the country. I never knew Fabio was involved with them. Muriel must have mentioned that I was a top scorer of my school team to Fabio.

When Dad found out that Fabio would be coming to Monday's training session, he decided to take the day off work for the event. Dad never comes to training sessions.

Suddenly I'll have two father figures watching over my footballing endeavours.

Dad has been going for lots of job interviews to try and get a different job. He keeps saying he hopes to work closer to home soon. So that he can come to all of my football training sessions.

I can't wait to see Fabio again.

After my disastrous trip to Hampden Stadium, I thought my chances of seeing any live footballers in action were zero. It just goes to show you should never give up hope. The game's not over until the referee (or Fabio, in this case) blows the whistle to halt all action.

Preparation for VIP Visit

Monday's football training session is only 5 days away. So I have substantially upped my daily training regime.

I have decided that each day until then I shall:-

- Eat 3 bowls of cereal for breakfast instead of 1.

154

- Do 30 Press ups (instead of the usual 20).

- Perform 40 laps of jogging round garden (instead of 30).

- Practise penalty shoot outs 30 times.

- Play football every day after school with Mikey (this is not far from the norm).

- Play football as much as possible with Dad (when here).

- Try my hardest at my Eastwood Rovers match this Saturday to emulate top premier league footballers' skills and score lots of goals.

- Have my hair cut again. To ensure my spikes look as pointy as possible. And that I look as much like Fabio's son-in-waiting as I can.

Star Player

Monday's football training session finally arrives.

We set off to collect Gran at 5.30 pm. She didn't want to miss out on attending the star event. There was a buzz of excitement in the air as all my family (Mum,

Dad, Melissa, Gran and I) travelled in our seven-seater silver car (which resembles a mini bus) to Eastwood Park Playing Fields where the training practice takes place.

I worry that my legs will be too shaky with excitement to score a goal in front of Fabio. Gran told me she felt jittery before piano exams as a child. But as soon as she started playing the nerves evaporated. I'm not sure that Gran's memory is that reliable. Especially going so far back. But I hoped all the same that that would happen to my nerves when I kicked the ball today.

The car park at Eastwood Park Playing Fields was jam-packed. So it took Dad ages to find a parking space. In fact, he got so fed up with us hurrying him to *"Park anywhere!"... "Fabio's waiting!"... "Hurry up, Dad!"...* that he abandoned our silver minibus on a grassy verge, muttering "Hold your horses it's not royalty we're meeting you know. He's only a football player."

"Only a football player!" I squealed. "We're talking about the captain of the best football team on the planet here. A tad jealous by any chance, DAD?"

Dad laughed. Finally relaxed now that no-one was pestering him. "Yes majorly jealous – of his pay packet!"

Mum and Gran chortled in agreement.

We all tumbled out of the people-carrier to find a sea of people swamping the playing field. In fact the crowd is so large that it extended right back to the car park itself.

News must have spread that a sporting legend was in the vicinity. (Mum must have been on another one

of her phoning/texting/facebooking/tweeting/emailing rampages.) Instead of the usual handful of loyal dads ready to cheer on their sporty sons, there was a massive throng of expectants fans chanting,
"Fabio! Fabio! Fabio!"

I spotted Muriel first.

Initially, I was confused as she had her plump lips covered in a bright pink lipstick this time and her blonde curly hair was tied up in a bunch.
This made her looked more yummy-mummy than film star beautiful. But she looked gorgeous nevertheless.
She was wearing a pink coat, to match her lipstick perhaps, and snugly-fitted jeans and furry brown boots.
Muriel held tightly onto the hand of a little boy who looked completely overwhelmed by the noisy crowd.
She directed Fabio with her free hand through the crammed car park towards the playing field.
I don't think a pop star would have received a more frenzied, star struck reception from the gathered masses.
Fabio waved and greeted his fans.
He signed autographs for those who had brought posters, books (although I noted NOT body parts) to sign. Muriel scoured the crowd until she caught sight of me gawping at them.

Her pretty face lit up no doubt with relief as well as pleasure when she spotted me and my family waving and gesturing for them to come over and join us.

Muriel dutifully pointed out where were in the huge cheering crowd to Fabio.

(In fact we remained right next to our silver car in the car park. It was so crowded we had not managed to move a tense, eagerly-awaiting-a-fun-game-of-football muscle.)

Fabio strode confidently through the group of fans that had gathered all around him, right over to **ME!!!**

I thought my already tight chest muscles might burst with pride as my beloved idol shook my hand, as all the other jealous schoolboys eagerly looked on.

Fabio had a warm, friendly smile.

He looked completely different not wearing his football strip.

He was however dressed in the official Super Strikers blue fleece coat (the one I had pestered Mum and Dad to buy me but to no avail due to its price tag of over £90) and jeans. His spiky hair looked even more impressive up close and I wondered what type of gel he used.

"Dexter, I've heard all about you from Muriel," he greeted me enthusiastically, placing his hand on my shoulder and standing back slightly to take in the sight of me, in all my glory. "What a little star in the making you are – and so funny, Muriel tells me!"

My lips wouldn't move to speak.

"What a legend you are, trying to invade the pitch and speak to me when you won those VIP tickets!" He laughed. "All my team mates were so impressed that I had such a loyal fan – willing to give up a premier seat at Super League game to meet me."

The whole Super Strikers team knew about me! Fabio thought I was a legend! Why is my mouth still refusing to operate and allow speech?

"Did you enjoy the bits of the match that you saw?" Fabio asked, obviously waiting for me to say something.

I nodded and omitted a strange squeaky noise that I tried to style out as a "Sure!"

Why did I feel so shy? I'm finally meeting my hero and I'm making a fool of myself.

C'mon Dex pull yourself together, boy!

"Great! Well, son, looks like your training's about to start. I hear you're quite the little goal scorer. Let 'em have it!" He encouraged me, ruffling my hair.

I'd tried to spike up to look exactly like his and was probably now ruined.

I didn't mind though.

FABIO HAD TOUCHED MY HAIR!

"Thanks," I finally managed some clear speech. Well as clear as you can be whilst grinning from ear to ear.

Son! Son! Fabio has just called me HIS son!

"I'll do my best." I tried to sound calm and sure of myself. After my earlier babyish, stuttering silence.

I sprinted off through the crowd to find Mikey and whispered in his ear, "Do you know what Fabio just called me? **SON!**"

"No way!" exclaimed Mikey.

"I know. All my dreams are coming true at once Mikey. C'mon, can't let the old man down!" I joked.

We raced over to join our coach and the rest of the team.

They were gathered at the side of the pitch, eagerly waiting for me to join them and fill them in on all of Fabio's news.

My heart was soaring, stealing breath from my lungs. My blood was pumping at super-speed, ready for the up and coming match.

FABIO had ruffled my hair.

FABIO had said that I was a superstar.

FABIO called me his son.

I was well and truly and star struck.

I had to concentrate hard on the coach's pep talk. And play the performance of my life.

Playing For Fabio

"Son"..."Son"..."Son"...

Fabio's words ran through my head faster than the opposing team's lead striker.

Fabio knows.

He knows that we belong together. Like father and son.

Thankfully my legs operated better than my lips did in front of Fabio. I managed once of my best performances to date at training. The first half of our Monday night training sessions always consists of lots of drills.

<u>I am pleased to report</u> –
- I never lost my breath during warm up star jumps

- My practice passes to and from Mikey were clean

- My dribbles never touched the cones

- I scored all of my penalty shoot outs, and

- I sprinted faster than all of the boys during running trials.

In the second half of training we had match play as usual.

Only nothing felt usual about this historic day.

We were split into two teams with black and white bibs respectively.

I managed to score three goals for my team *(The Whites)*. Beating TB who was playing for the opposing side. He managed to put away a valiant *two* goals.

TB was showing off like mad in front of Fabio.

He did all but perform a double backflip.

Unfortunately for TB, he was so busy trying to catch Fabio's eye (that was loyally trained on me, much to TB's resentment) that he inadvertently hacked the leg of Billy Mandleson. Billy was playing in defence for *my* team. This caused Billy to trip. And hurt his shoulder as he landed at an awkward angle.

A penalty was awarded to The Whites.

I bravely stepped forward to take on the challenge...

Thankfully, the goalie dived the completely wrong way so I managed to pop the ball in...

To an almighty roar from the crowd!

I had been so focused on my game and not letting myself down in front of *Fabio* that this was the first juncture in the game that I allowed myself to look up and drink in the atmosphere.

It was such an amazing feeling to have a massive gathering like this cheering you on.

My eyes were drawn to where my family was standing. I spotted Melissa high up on Dad's shoulders, cheering me on. Mum was clapping. And Dad was whooping at me. Gran looked proud as punch as she gave me a little encouraging wave.

I allowed myself a little unprofessional half-wave back. Fabio, Muriel and the little boy were smiling and clapping and seemed to be enjoying the match too.

When the final whistle blew it was 6-2 to our team.

I'd won my first match in front of Fabio. Although strangely it was my own family that I was most pleased to have made proud.

It was rare to have Mum and Gran at a match. And Dad never usually watches my training. It goes without saying that Melissa would rather dye her hair blue than watch football. But we were all united on this occasion.

I was awarded Man of the Match by our coach (probably more for bringing Fabio to our training grounds than my play). Mikey lifted me onto his shoulders briefly, before collapsing to the ground due to the considerable weight of my strong muscles.

I could have done no more to impress Fabio.

The Aftermath

Immediately after training, Fabio bounded over to where I was standing with my family...with *his* family.

"Well done, Dexter! What a penalty – straight in the back of the net. The goalie never even got a touch of the ball."

"Cheers," I mumbled modestly.

"This is my son, Sammy," said Fabio, finally introducing me to the little boy who had arrived with Muriel and him. "He's only four but he's already got a strong kick! Loves footie already don't you Sam?"

Sammy nodded. He was so cute, all wrapped up in his blue puffy jacket and warm woollen mittens.

He was wearing the latest Super Strikers woolly hat. The same one that I had got at Christmas-time. Only his was much smaller of course. Some dark chocolate brown curls peeked out from under his warm hat. He stared up at me with his large hazel brown eyes. His skin was a tan colour. And he had those adorable puffy cheeks that little kids always have. Sam was holding on tightly to a furry chipmunk toy, a replica of the Super Striker mascot.

He's so lucky. I'd love one of those!

"Hi Sammy, sounds like you might grow up to be a footballer like your Dad!" I greeted him, smiling broadly at his chubby grin. "You're so lucky to have the best coach in the whole world in your very own family"

Fabio chipped in, "I hardly ever get a chance to play football with Sammy, Dex. I'm either training. Or having physio. To make sure my muscles don't get fatigued. After that's done, I just to want to relax. Or play golf with the lads. Helps me to switch off from constantly thinking about football. And up and coming fixtures."

I was stunned. Fabio hardly ever played football with his own son.

"I play footie with Dad all the time in my garden. Admittedly I have to pester him a bit. But he always agrees," I told Fabio.

"Good for you Mr Hunter," Fabio shook Dad's hand warmly. "Your coaching skills are obviously paying off. You've got a professional player in the making there."

Dad was taken aback by such praise and spluttered, "I'm sure it's not *my* coaching skills that have paid off. But all Dexy's hard work. He's never out of that garden training – loves it, so he does."

"Obsessed," agreed Mum.

"Just as it should be," confirmed Fabio.

Muriel who had been chatting on her mobile phone finished her call and joined in the conversation. "Well

165

done Dexter – you were superb. I'm so glad Fabio got a chance to watch you."

"You were right, love. He's a one off," smiled Fabio, putting his arm around Muriel's waist.

Love? Canoodling in front of strangers?

As if reading my mind - we must be so alike that we're telepathic - Fabio asked if I remembered Muriel interviewing me for the Super League Bulletin.

"Of course – you had red lipstick on that day," I blurted out like a fool.

Luckily everyone laughed.

Muriel fished out a bit of paper from her handbag and passed it to me.

"I forgot to bring this to my interview. It's a copy of the winning entry for the *GOAL Magazine* competition. *GOAL* submitted it to us when they were applying for your VIP seats at the Super League game. It's very artistic and a good likeness of Fabio."

She gazed adoringly at Fabio as if to reassure herself that he was indeed as gorgeous as I'd made him look in the picture.

I beamed proudly.

"Thanks, my friend Mikey was a big help." I looked around for Mikey to share our moment of glory. But he was miles away taking photos of us chatting with Fabio, from the excellent vantage point of the top of the grassy hill beside the training field. Ever the true friend. I couldn't wait to see how those snaps turned out. He gave me the thumbs up sign when he saw me looking over.

"I'll need to try and meet your friend Mikey before I go," said Fabio.

"I don't think you'll have time unfortunately," said Muriel examining her watch which was difficult to read in the dark winter evening light.

"It's nearly eight o'clock. Well past Sammy's bedtime. And the traffic will be in gridlock, no doubt."

"Really, is that the time?" Fabio checked his watch. "Well Dexter, it's been a real privilege to meet you. I would say don't try and invade the pitch again to meet me but I don't need to worry about that from now on."

"Since I've already met you?" I asked.

He leaned in and whispered conspiratorially. "No, it's because I'm off to play for Barca next season. Rumours have been circulating in all the papers. But I guess you're too young to read those."

"You're going to be leaving Scotland?" I asked astonished. Fabio had lived here since he was a little child.

"Yes, I've been at the Edinburgh Sharpes since I was fifteen. So I feel it's time for a change, Dex. Also my parents are from Barcelona. And will be retiring back there next year. So we'll all be together which will be lovely."

I tried to hide my disappointment and look pleased for him.

167

"The Sharpes will be lost without you." I managed.
Of course, meaning *I* would be lost without him.
Without my dreams of him becoming my coach and
joining my family.

"I'm sure the Sharpes will have some young
whipper snapper lined up to replace me. Maybe it'll be
you one day."

Fabio winked at me.

His complement lightened my mood so I couldn't
resist quipping, "Maybe you'll come back and be my
coach one day."

Fabio's head tilted back as he let out a deep throaty
laugh, "You're a hoot, Dex. I just love you. I bet
coaching you would be loads of fun. I'll definitely bare
it in mind. Once I hang my playing boots up once and
for all. Although I can't guarantee that the freezing
cold and rain will be pulling me back from the Spanish
sunshine. But you never know Dexy. So long, son. It
was lovely to meet you."

I actually found myself blinking back the tears as
Fabio gave me a hug goodbye.

His impending departure had come as such a
shock.

Sensing this, Muriel gave my upper arm a little
squeeze and said, "Well you can either support Barca
now, Dex. Or find some other footballer to idolise!"

168

Muriel explained that Sammy was tired since his bedtime was 7 pm so this was a late night for him. Fabio had wanted him to come along and join in the fun. She held up Sammy's hand for him and gave it a little shake by way of a floppy, sleepy goodbye from him.

Muriel said her goodbyes to everyone. Fabio made a point of shaking hands with all of my family, including me, before he left. So polite.

My family waved him off respectfully, as he made his way back to his car.

My ears were reeling with the news of Fabio planning to leave Scotland next season, long after he had left our training ground.

As Fabio's red soft-top sports car zoomed away, I felt as though the whole evening had been a dream.

Surely I hadn't just played football in front of Fabio Galianto and met his whole family.

Surely he hadn't just told me that he was leaving Edinburgh to play for Barcelona in the summer.

Surely he wasn't going to be a traitor and LEAVE!

Fabio had driven off, along with my dreams of him becoming my coach and companion any time soon.

It would be a long time until Fabio hung up his boots. A legend like that.

169

Some top players still play professional football in their mid-thirties.

By the time Fabio is thirty-five, I'll be in my late twenties. Obviously by then I'll already be earning millions playing for a top Premier League football club.

By then it'll be way too late for his services!

The thought of no longer trying to impress Fabio, or badger him to become my coach, was in a strange way a relief.

I no longer had to win the attention of Fabio.

I could play my best football, train my hardest and make myself and my own family proud. In fact the Hunter clan already seemed pretty impressed with the way the evening had gone so far. It was pretty cool of them *ALL* to come out and support me on this cold magical winter evening.

Within minutes of Fabio's departure, all that remained in my thoughts was how impressive his hair looked up close. It was such a unique style.

As soon as I got home, I planned to go to my bedroom mirror and try and create a new unique look for myself - the sort little boys like Sammy might try and emulate in the future.

Journey Home

In the car, on the short drive home, I felt drained all of a sudden.

It was as if all my energy had seeped out of my body into my Nike football boots.

My legs were leaden.

I was covered in mud from diving for every ball that came my way.

My spirits remained high though.

It was only on the drive home, as I relaxed and recovered from the match, that I glanced down at the picture that Muriel had handed me.

"There's been some mistake," I said quietly. "This winning picture that Muriel gave me. It isn't the drawing that Mikey and I did."

"What's that you said, Dex?" asked Dad peering at me in the rear-view car mirror.

"The winning picture that Muriel handed me... it's not mine. I stuck ping pong balls onto mine. Remember all that bother you had trying to post it, Mum?"

"I certainly remember the long queue at the post office that day!"

After a brief pause, "It's my picture," piped up Melissa.

"*Yours?*" the entire population of the car enquired in unison.

Melissa and I are not famous for our brother and sisterly cooperation.

"I was sick of you watching football on the TV for hours on end. I thought that if you got the chance to go to a live match, it would give me some peace. To watch some of my favourite programmes for once. Or do something fun with just mum. Like ice skating or baking."

I examined Melissa's picture closely.

Very surprised that my little sister had engineered the whole thing.

Mel had drawn Fabio in a sombrero hat sitting on top of a donkey on a sunny beach in Spain. He was sticking out his foot to kick a beach ball and tickling a sunbather in the tummy with his other foot. Melissa had obviously used her fancy gel pens.

The whole picture sparkled and seemed to jump of the page.

"Here, this is pretty good. I can see why it won. You've got a good likeness of Fabio. And the picture's so sparkly and colourful."

"That's why I borrowed your posters. I was leaning in close to copy Fabio's face accurately. That's how I accidentally got a few pen marks on the posters," Melissa explained.

I couldn't believe it.

"No way – gosh I'm so sorry Melissa. I'll never doubt you again. I may be a true fan of Fabio but you are more than a true sister to me," I replied solemnly.

"Cheers, Dex!" She grinned before adding, "Well you are hopeless at drawing Dexter and would never have won a drawing competition, let's face it!"

The car peeled with laughter. Melissa was spot on. My family knew me so well.

END OF SEASON ROUND UP

April/May Highlights

When his contract with the Edinburgh Sharpes expired, at the end of the season, Fabio announced that he was leaving as captain of Super Strikers. He finally told the world what I already knew – that he would be moving to his parent's home team of Barca in Spain in July.

This caused equal measures of joy to the Barca fans and disappointment to the Scottish fans. If it hadn't been for Fabio quietly explaining his feelings to me at my training match, I would have been bereft.

However once the news sunk in, a fellow sportsman like me understood the need for a challenge. I knew it was a top move for Fabio. And decided to back him all the way. You never know, maybe I'll get a chance to see him live in action out in Spain some time.

Well a boy can dream can't he?

The Super Strikers won the Super League 2010/11 by 7 games to 3. Fabio (who else?) scored 21 goals and proudly received the Star Footballer of the Year gold medal. He dedicated it to all the young aspiring footballers in Scotland *(surely he meant me?)*. Fabio donated his prize money to a charity called *Let's Get Moving* that provides sports equipment to underprivileged areas of Scotland.

Eastwood Rovers finished top place in the Schools Football League. We got our picture in three papers: the school newsletter, our local paper and also Edinburgh's leading newspaper, The Scotsman. *Mum was very proud.*

My Total Goals scored for the season amounted to 46. 4 more than last year's 42-goal tally. But 4 short of my 50 goal target, due to my unfortunate football bans. Thankfully it was enough to make me the **top scorer**

for The Edinburgh School Football League 2011/12. TB, who achieved even more football bans than me, only managed 39 goals this season. I was mentioned in all three newspaper articles. *I felt like a champion!*

On 29th April, I was approached by the Scottish Football Development Agency's Director of Young Talent. They asked me to join their training programme for **talented young footballers in Scotland**. The football traineeship offers the best coaching in the country apparently (now that Fabio's left for Spain presumably!). The scouts had spotted the article about me in The Scotsman. Mikey was right about playing well being the simplest way to be spotted. What did my Research Topic in November say... **if you're good enough you'll get spotted!!!**

On 27th April, Melissa entered an Easter drawing competition at the local shopping arcade. She achieved **first place** winning a giant chocolate Easter egg, a fluffy bunny and £50 vouchers to spend at the shopping centre. Just rewards for all her hard work. *Good on you, Mel!*

On 18th May, Dad announced his top transfer news. He would be leaving Manchester to start a new job in Edinburgh in a month's time! The pay offer was good apparently. The accountancy team that he would be leading are all excellent players, if a little lacking in personality Dad advises. *It's the best transfer news ever!*

Dexter's Results Table

Season's Goal:
Fabio to become my Coach & Companion

1. Fabio To Become My Coach:

Not scored. *Sadly.*
Although may pop in a late goal in extra time once Fabio is retired!

2. Fabio To Become My Companion:

Scored!
Fabio has...
- watched me play football
- met my family
- introduced me to his family, including his wife and little son
- shared his private transfer news with me.

I've definitely made a friend for life...

Life Goal

To Become A Super League Player

I've followed Fabio's quote on how to become a
Super League star player all season.

Here's how I've got on:-

1. Natural Talent
Scored!

2. Expert Coaching
Scored!   Top coaches from the SFDA will now
train me FOUR times a week.

3. Childhood Dreams
Scored!   My journal's brimming with them.

4. Dedicated Practising
Scored!   Training's quadrupled, from Monday
nights alone to four times a week.

5. Follow The Game

Scored!   I've now got TWO leagues to follow -
the Spanish and the Super League.

<u>OVERALL RESULT:</u>

SCORED!!!